Tempting the Maiden

Book 3
Sherwood Forest Shifters

Anna Lowe

Contents

Free Books

Get your free e-books now!

Sign up for my newsletter at *annalowebooks.com* to get three free books!

- *Desert Wolf*: Friend or Foe (Book 1.1 in the Twin Moon Ranch series)

- *Off the Charts* (the prequel to the Serendipity Adventure series)

- *Perfection* (the prequel to the Blue Moon Saloon series)

Chapter One

TUCK

Nottingham, England

February 1194

I crept around the cliff's edge, letting my eyes adjust to the moon and starlight. The dry, sandy earth under my paws made it easy to blend into the landscape, and a brisk sea breeze toyed with strands of my thick mane. I looked left and right, then raced across open terrain to a rocky outcrop, my next point of cover. There, I crouched, belly to the ground, and tested the wind. I whisked my tufted tail back and forth. The enemy was out there, not far away.

Step by step, I advanced, letting my shoulders swing like powerful blades. I heard the faint crackle of campfires and the hushed voices of sentries far behind me, but I tuned them out. Those were my own comrades. My focus was the enemy.

I prowled forward, every sense piqued, knowing my next step could be my last — or could take me to glory.

Impatient, I picked up my pace, jogging, then sprinting to the shelter of a bluff. I took cover there, barely daring to breathe. My heart pounded, because it was a matter of minutes, maybe seconds, until the fight of my life. Then, with a quiet shake of my mane and a quick prayer, I bared my teeth and charged the enemy.

Cries sounded, and a dozen swords were drawn with metal *zings*. But they were all too late. I pounced, eviscerating the first man, then swatted away a second and slashed at a third.

One after another, the Ayyubids screamed and fell, while others ran for their lives. I roared and pursued them, vowing to chase them all the way back to...

A cow mooed, and I pulled up short. My breaths vaporized in the cold night air as reality slowly closed back in on me. *Puff... Puff... Puff...*

I hung my head, suddenly aware of the hard earth beneath the pads of my feet. The ground was frosty, not dry, the night cold and crisp. I wasn't in an advance party of King Richard's forces in the Crusades, and those weren't ferocious Ayyubid forces ahead of me, led by their crafty leader, Saladin. They were cows. And that heathen I'd eviscerated... I looked over the mess I'd made of the pumpkin patch, then hung my head.

Too bad I wasn't a wolf shifter instead of a lion. Then I could lift my muzzle and howl in misery.

I wasn't the knight I had always dreamed of being. I was a friar at Winslow Abbey.

I sat on the frozen ground of the country I'd never left, wishing I were anywhere and anyone else but me. If I'd been born first, like my eldest brother, I would have inherited the family's title, duties, and estate. Even better, if I'd been born second, I would have landed my dream job of knight. But fate had seen to it that I'd been born third and thus condemned me to the life of a priest.

I ran my claws along the ground, digging deep, frosty furrows. Then I raised my head and let out a silent scream, and another and another. So many, with so much anger and frustration, I could have wept.

And then I did.

Eventually, I dropped in a pitiful heap. Not king of the jungle, nor the land, nor even my own destiny. Just me.

Worse, even. I was a priest. Well, nearly. In a few short days, I would take my vows of poverty, chastity, and obedience and make it official.

Poverty...

No problem. As the son of a wealthy lord, it was only fair to make up for my privileged upbringing.

Obedience...

I made a face. Not my strong suit. If I'd been in an army, I could have lived with it. But it was hard to take orders from men who spoke in gentle whispers and dressed in bathrobes.

Chastity...

Big problem. I just didn't have it in me.

But that was my future, and damn, was that future bleak.

I tried the only thing I could to regain a sense of control over my life, at least while I was in lion form: grooming myself. I started with my haunches, then worked my way down each paw. One measured lick after another, I worked my fur back into place. Then I moistened one paw and focused on my cheeks, forehead, and ears.

But not even that helped. I gazed listlessly into the distance, letting my shoulders rise then fall in another huge sigh. Mark Tuckerton, the man I used to be, was well and truly gone. Now, I was just Tuck, and the highlight of my life was sneaking out of Winslow Abbey at night to pretend.

The only true satisfaction I felt these days came from helping Robynne Hood, but those occasions were few and far between. Too bad the woman was so damned competent. I might see more action that way.

Still, it was something, wasn't it?

At least, that's what I tried telling myself.

Chapter Two

TUCK

Slowly, I turned back for the abbey, resigned to another miserably quiet night. A lonely night, like so many others behind and so many more ahead of me. I stared glumly at the abbey — from the soaring church tower to the solid block of the dormitory, the refectory, the library...

At least there was that. As a friar, I wouldn't have to live my life within those four walls. Once I finished my training, I could live in any normal community.

The thought perked me up, and a new idea took root in my mind. Who said it had to be a normal community? What if I could join Robynne Hood's Merry Men in Sherwood Forest?

The abbot was responsible for assigning me to a certain location, but maybe I could work around that the same way I'd worked around so many unsavory duties in the monastery. Like library duty — day after backbreaking day hunched over a table, copying books word for word. I'd weaseled my way out of that, hadn't I? All it had taken were a few missed vowels... paragraphs... even chapters here and there. Not to mention the mustaches I'd added to the angels or fair ladies painted around the edges...

Then there'd been the job in the laundry — a metaphor for cleansing my soul, as Father Benjamin had lectured me on. I'd lasted less than three days, thanks to a lot of hot water that shrank the abbot's underpants down a few sizes. Which only made sense, as I'd told Father Benjamin. As a man of the cloth, the abbot didn't have much use for the equipment he kept down there anyway.

That had landed me in the kitchen, followed by a job with the herbalist — two laughably easy assignments to get myself booted from — to the brewery, a job I was much more suited to, with a side gig in the garden. Not as bad as I'd imagined, since it took me outdoors. Still, it was a long, long way from the exotic lands and valiant deeds I pined for.

I sighed. Once upon a time, my father had clapped me on the shoulder and said, *You'll know the day you become a man, my boy. You'll recognize it when the moment arrives.*

I snorted. I could live to one hundred in this abbey and never experience a challenge that brought me to that point. I would forever remain a misplaced soul shriveling slowly away.

I clawed at a tree, then continued toward the stables. When a mule brayed, I quickly shifted to human form.

"Shh," I called, giving Rita a pat. "Good girl."

She and Rosie were the only females at the abbey. Too bad they were both equines. Both were unwitting accomplices to my nightly forays in lion form since I left my clothes at their end of the stable.

Then I slapped a hand over my mouth. I was supposed to be observing a vow of silence. Did talking to mules count?

It was late — nearly midnight — and though I doubted anyone would spot me, I shushed them a second time. I pulled on my tunic and plain brown robe, then tied my belt, a simple length of rope.

See? Poverty, I could do, easily. Didn't one out of three count for something?

I ran my hands over my hair, patting it into place. One strand, then another, and another...

Okay, so the feline in me liked to look good. But if it was my lion side, it didn't really qualify as vanity. More like a basic need, like food, water, and air to breathe.

Rita nickered softly, and some of the horses stirred in their stalls — including the pretty white mare across the aisle. A classy new arrival who seemed out of place among all the beasts of burden around her.

Good night, ladies, I mouthed to them all. *See you tomorrow.*

Rita and Rosie nickered as I flicked my hood over my straw-colored hair and stole across the lawn. I paused under the arched entrance of the monastery, then slipped inside. I was halfway up the long staircase to the dormitory when it hit me. I'd forgotten to do one thing.

I backtracked down the stairs, happy for a little excitement, as minor as it was.

Tuck, please, you have to help me. Cyril, one of the other novices, had begged me earlier that evening.

I tiptoed down the hallway and out into the arched colonnade of the cloister, keeping to the deepest shadows. A fountain bubbled in the center of the garden, the only sound in the abbey at that late hour.

I need you to sneak into the library, Cyril had continued.

Easy, my lion hummed.

I hurried from one column to the next, paused, then hurried on. Each was chiseled with a different motif: a saint here, a shield there, and even a few mythical creatures...or not so mythical, like the dragon wrapped around the next column.

Dragons, my lion sniffed. *So high and mighty, and such attitudes.*

Moving silently, I pushed open a heavy door and entered the chapter house. Normally a place for meetings, it was eerily quiet at this late hour. I headed for the stairs in the right corner, leading to the second level.

If I hadn't been on a secret mission, I would have taken the broad, straight stairs at the other end of the building. But this back staircase was a better option for a man sneaking around like a burglar. I kept my head cocked as I wound around and around the spiral staircase, keeping my eyes and ears peeled for trouble.

I left behind a few doodles, Cyril had explained, wringing his hands and turning red. *The kind with no place in a book on holy subjects.*

I grinned. Cyril wasn't just the abbey's best singer — he was also the best illustrator in the scriptorium, where the library's most precious books were laboriously copied. But like the rest of us novices, he suffered from an overactive, unquenched libido.

Some of the guys took those urges out on themselves. Some took them out on one another. That made sense, though I wasn't thus inclined — or that desperate. Yet. My not-too-satisfying solution was vivid fantasies in my bed at night, reliving every sweet kiss, every heated touch of my former life — and adding in a hefty dose of my own imagination.

Art was Cyril's form of release, though I doubted the abbot would call it that. I'd snuck a peek at Cyril's doodles once and had a good chuckle. Mostly, they showed naked men and women getting it on in bed, though the details showed Cyril was working more from imagination than experience. Not unless he knew some really wild positions that would make even a sex-starved acrobat balk.

Those were the sketches he'd left behind earlier in the day. But Cyril didn't have the nerve to sneak across the abbey at night, so he'd begged me to retrieve them for him. A rescue mission, you could say, even if it wasn't the kind I'd once imagined.

I paused at the entry to the scriptorium, getting my bearings. Three rows of four desks each, all nice and tidy. A can at the upper right corner of each held quills, blotters, and brushes, with a cubby under each desk for scraps of parchment. I went to the third desk on the right and started riffling through it.

The scriptorium had the biggest windows in the abbey for lighting by day. Even now, at night, they admitted enough moonlight to help me make out the drawings. The first scrap had a sketch of a letter S, its curves populated by rows of lords and ladies. The next was a B filled with pretty lilies. Then came a corner with a lady petting a unicorn, and at the bottom, a saint hacking at a giant snail.

I chuckled. Now, that was an artist I could relate to.

I flipped through more sheets, pausing only to snort at a poorly drawn lion. Unless the image was intended to capture a lion shifter in the process of transforming, his features were far too human. And what self-respecting feline would go around sticking out his tongue like that?

I saw it all — animals, plants, and mythological creatures. But no bedroom antics.

If they're not in my desk, they must be with the project I was working on, Cyril had said. *They might have gotten mixed in with the papers Father Benedict gathered up to bring upstairs to the library. Oh God! If anyone finds them...*

I headed back to the spiral staircase and up to the next level, all in pitch dark. Working mostly by feel, I finally emerged on a tiny landing with a window just big enough to let in a sliver of light. The library's back door was locked, but I'd been at the abbey long enough to feel along the upper frame for the key. Seconds later, the door clicked, and I pushed it open, entering the library.

I grinned, because my secret mission was feeling more secret than ever, and my adrenaline was kicking in — a first for me, at least in a library.

I headed for a table I could just make out in the dim light, but I never got there. And I didn't catch the shadow rushing in at me from the right until it was too late. A split second later, I was shoved against the stone wall and pinned there, with my arms yanked painfully behind my back.

A lock of silky black hair fell over my shoulder and tickled my cheek. Then a blade pricked my neck, and someone hissed, "Move, and you're dead."

I went limp, playing along just long enough to lull my attacker into a false sense of security. Then I spun out of his grip and slammed him against the wall. The knife clattered away on the stone floor. I pinned him there the exact way he'd held me, with my elbow against his back to be doubly secure. Then it was my turn to lean in close and hiss in his ear.

"Move, and you're dead."

It had all gone so quickly, my senses didn't catch up until a split second later. Then my nostrils flared, and my thoughts blurred at her heavenly flowers-in-a-meadow scent.

Then my mind caught up with my nose, and I frowned. Wait. *Her* scent?

My lion hummed. *Yes*, her. *A woman.*

Chapter Three

MARIAN

The attacker was twice my weight and at least a head taller than me. No matter how much I kicked or struggled, I couldn't get free.

Then he hesitated and loosened his grip. Twisting out of his arms, I yanked my spare knife out of my sleeve. I held it between us, practically baring my teeth.

"Get your hands off me!"

He blinked, then fanned the space between us. "Um... they are off you."

I scowled. A minor technicality.

I'd only had a few candles burning, but they illuminated his fair hair like golden flax under the summer sun. The little bit of moonlight that snuck through the windows found his amber eyes, making them glow.

"Well, your hands were on me a second ago," I snipped. When he raised an eyebrow, I cursed myself. That came out all wrong.

"Um... apologies?" he offered.

I pulled myself to my full height. Which only brought me to his shoulder, drat the man. His square jaw was directly before me, speckled with stubble the same color as his hair. My gaze jumped to the universe in his eyes, then drifted lower, lingering on his chiseled cheeks, his perfect lips, then down his neck. One layered with just enough muscle to hint at how the rest of him was built.

I gave myself a little shake. "What gave you the right to grab me in the first place?"

"You grabbed me first." Then he winced and slapped a hand over his mouth.

I stared. What was up with this man?

All my life, I'd been prepared for a kidnapping/murder scenario, just in case. Twice, that scenario had actually played out, and I'd had to fight for my life. I'd also been accosted by men in several less-dangerous situations. But never had I encountered a man so...so...

I searched for the word. Strange? Unpredictable?

Handsome, a sultry voice purred in the back of my mind.

True, with hair as fair as mine was dark and eyes as bright as mine were black.

"What?" I finally demanded.

He moved his hand. "It's just..." Then he covered his mouth again and murmured through his fingers. "Dang. I broke it. Again."

Definitely the strangest assassin I'd ever encountered.

"Broke what?"

"My vow of silence."

I pointed at his hand. "I'm quite certain talking is talking, even if you do it through your fingers."

Then I cursed myself. Why was I even indulging this lunatic?

He slumped. "You're right. Not much point in keeping it up, I guess." Then he sighed. "Until they make me take the vow again, I suppose."

Who was *they*? Who was he?

He was dressed as a monk, but it had to be the worst disguise I'd ever seen. The robes might fit him, but they certainly didn't suit him, and he wore them as comfortably as I might wear a stiff, high-necked dress.

I sniffed surreptitiously, then froze. It wasn't just his profession he was hiding. The man was a shifter, too. Some kind of feline, if I wasn't mistaken.

How did I know? Well, I had my secrets too.

"Stay back," I warned when he reached out.

He yanked his hand back. "I am. I mean, I will. I mean, sorry."

Polite for an assassin, but really, what was the point?

His eyes crossed a little as he focused on the point of my blade. Pretty cute, I couldn't help noting.

"You're good with a knife." He waved toward my dagger.

I glowed. How nice to be acknowledged for a skill I'd worked so hard to develop.

Then he ruined it all by blurting, "And, wow. You're beautiful."

I brandished the dagger, doubly angry, but somehow, he didn't seem to notice.

"You fight dirty, too." He nodded in approval.

"You don't?"

"I prefer to talk dirty." He chuckled, then caught himself. "Bad joke, sorry. It's just that I've been here so long..." He gave himself a shake, making that blond mane sway. "Not a good excuse."

With a sigh, he turned back to the wall and stuck his arms behind his back. Now what was he doing?

"Sorry again," he said, though the words were muffled by the wall.

I stared. What now?

"Go ahead." He wiggled his arms against his back. "Do what you must. I deserve the worst."

It was definitely some kind of trick. I had to beware.

But that was hard, and getting harder all the time, because something about him drew me in, whispering, *You can trust me.*

We can trust him, my second self agreed.

A voice somewhere deep in my soul echoed the message more ominously. *You* must *trust him.*

Then I came to my senses. I couldn't trust anyone, especially not with family secrets no one could ever discover.

I nearly backed away, worried he might somehow pick up my scent. Unlikely, given how faint and unusual it was. Most people — even shifters — put it down to a flowery perfume.

Instead, I succumbed to temptation and inched closer. Close enough to kiss, technically, but with the point of my blade grazing his back instead.

His broad, muscled back. Between that and the notion of a *kiss*, my knees wobbled a little bit.

"Go on," he urged.

Kiss him? Kill him? Which did he mean?

"Go on with what?" I demanded.

"Whatever you were going to do once you subdued me."

I frowned. Frankly, I hadn't thought that far ahead. All the self-defense plans I'd learned counted on screaming to bring guards running to my defense. That, or I was supposed to run for it. But I was exactly where I wanted to be. Why would I leave?

I stepped back, keeping my dagger ready. "Who are you? What do you want here?"

He turned slowly, and whoa. That face was definitely wasted in a monastery. The hard, muscled body too. He ought to be off crusading with my godfather, the king.

"I'm Tuck."

"Tuck who?"

He shrugged. "Just Tuck. I'm a monk. Well, training to be."

"Ha. I don't believe that for a minute. You've been sent by Prince John, haven't you?"

He cocked his head. "Sent by Prince John to...?" Then his jaw went all hard, even angry. "Wait. Are you in danger? Is he after you?"

His voice went a little hopeful, like he'd been waiting years for a fair maiden to rescue.

Well, no thank you. I didn't wait, and I certainly didn't need to be rescued.

Then his eyes went wide, and he got even more excited. "Have you been locked up here?"

God, men and their *brave knight* complexes!

I stuck my hands on my hips. "No, I am not locked up. Even if I were, do you really think I'd leave my fate to a random man arriving at the right place and time to save me? And he'd have no strings attached, of course. Only my hand in marriage and entrapment as his bedmate forever."

He blinked. "Oh. Never thought of that."

I snorted. "Are you a good liar, or are you from a different planet?"

He scratched his head. "I think a monastery must count as a different planet."

There he went again, deflecting my argument. Still, I kept up my guard. Men wanted to possess, to claim. To use and abuse as they saw fit. Of course, there were exceptions, but those were so rare, it was best to put strangers in that ninety-nine-percent category.

"I swear, I'm a monk," he continued. "Not by choice, maybe..."

I rolled my eyes. "You're not exactly building a strong argument."

"You know, you're very confusing."

Ha. There went the pot, calling the kettle black.

"The door was locked," he pointed out, still pursuing his ridiculous *maidens need rescuing* theory.

I pointed to a big bronze key on a nearby table. "From the inside. But maybe I'll push a desk against the door from now on, just in case."

He put up his hands. "I'm not here to hurt you."

"No? Then you're roaming the halls of the abbey at midnight to...?"

He gestured to a desk. "I'm here for some sketches."

I frowned. He really was insane. The library was full of priceless treasures, from centuries-old Bibles to dusty artworks. Yet all he wanted were some sketches?

This was definitely the nuttiest lion, tiger, or leopard shifter I'd ever met.

Lion, I decided. First, they were more common in this part of the world, and second, they were the chattiest of the great cats.

"What sketches?"

He grinned, waggling his eyebrows. "Ones a fair lady probably oughtn't see."

I rolled my eyes. "Oh yes. As a fair lady, I must be protected from many things. Bloody wounds. Naked bodies. Sex."

He looked a little stunned that I'd uttered that three-letter word but quickly recovered.

"Well, if you want to see them..."

I threw up my hands. "No, I do not want to see them. And I'm scandalized that you do."

He shook his head vehemently. "I need them for a friend!"

"Ha. I bet."

"Truly!"

The crazy thing was, I found myself wanting to believe him. To trust him. To learn more about him.

"Looking at indecent art isn't a good hobby for someone who chose the priesthood," I observed.

"It's not my hobby. And I'm not here by choice, believe me." He plucked glumly at his brown robe. "The only part I like is the hood."

He flipped it up, giving himself a *dangerous assassin* look. But when he flipped it down again, his broad grin made me picture...

"You'd make a better minstrel than monk," I observed.

"I'd make an even better knight." He stretched to his full height, making it awfully convincing.

"So what are you doing here?"

"You know... third son and all that."

Ah. Right. In the tradition of landed gentry, the first son inherited the family's title, land, and wealth. The second son was expected to become a knight and bring glory to the family name through brave deeds. Unlucky number three was destined for life in a monastery. If I'd had brothers instead of being an only child, the same would have applied to my family.

Then he cocked his head. "So, that's my excuse. What are you doing here?"

"Just a visitor in search of spiritual guidance."

He cackled. "Well, good luck. I've been here six months and haven't found any."

"Then maybe that's not what you're looking for."

He took a long, quiet minute to digest that, then let out a soft, defeated sigh. "Tell that to the abbot."

Briefly, he drifted into sorrow and self-pity. But that obviously wasn't in his character, because he bounced right back to upbeat and curious. His eyes roved the room, taking in the daybed I'd been slumbering on to the few belongings I'd brought, so out of place in the library.

"The abbey has a guest room. And yet you're up here."

"I like reading."

A tiny smile played over his lips. "I suppose you must. And needlepoint." He pointed to the project I'd left beside the bed.

"*She is clothed...*" He started reading in the dim light, then glanced up, waggling his eyebrows.

I rolled my eyes. That was as far as I'd gotten. "*She is clothed with strength and dignity,*" I finished, exasperated.

He grinned. "And a hell of a dagger."

"Not just one, so watch it."

In truth, the needlepoint was a decoy, making people believe I was a helpless damsel.

Ha. Let them believe, an inner voice jeered.

I shushed that hidden side of myself and gestured to the door with my dagger. "Time for you to go, Mister Tuck."

He seemed to rejoice in the *Mister* part. Maybe the same way I rejoiced when people left out *Maid* before my name. *Marian* suited me so much better than that haughty, virginal *Maid Marian.*

Tuck nodded. "I suppose it is. But I really need to get those sketches first."

"Right. For your friend." I emphasized the last word.

He went pink. It suited him.

"I swear they're not mine."

"And they're for entertainment, I assume? Or are you going to try to convince me they're educational?"

He broke into a broad smile. "Maybe a little entertaining. But mostly, I'm here to keep a friend out of trouble."

Short, simple words, but somehow, they spoke volumes. He might believe in outdated notions about frail, helpless women, but his heart was in the right place when it came to helping others. So maybe being a monk suited him.

A second later, I stifled a laugh. No. *Knight* was definitely more fitting.

I motioned to a large table cluttered with papers. "Be my guest."

He scurried over, holding one scrap after another up to the light. I started out watching him like a hawk but soon found myself helping him. Why? Maybe the thrill of the chase. Or maybe my competitive side liked the idea of beating him to the discovery. Or just plain curiosity.

Either way, I dropped my defenses. Rightly so, because Tuck truly seemed intent on a more innocent mission than I'd assumed.

"Got them!" he called out, holding some papers to the light.

I scurried over for a look, but he held them higher, laughing. "I'm not sure you want to see this."

"I'll be the judge of that."

He turned one way then the other, making me pivot with him. Every time I grabbed for the papers, my hands brushed his body. More than once, my torso did too.

"Give me that," I insisted, laughing.

"I will not."

"You will too."

He raised the sketches high, then jerked them low, out of my reach. Just like the ball games I'd played with my cousin when I was little. Fun games. Innocent games. Games that got your heart pumping and your body sweating.

"This is definitely not for your eyes," he laughed, holding the sketches out of reach.

I got on tippy-toes, grasping for them. "If you're worried about protecting my virtue, don't. It's too late for that."

His eyes went wide. Oops. Not the kind of thing a proper young lady ought to admit. It did give me a chance to snatch the sketches, though.

"Ha!" I cheered, then turned my back to him to study them.

He reached over my shoulder, but I ducked away. "No, you don't. These are..." I turned the sketch the right way up, then stared. "Oh. My."

He laughed. "Told you so."

The room went quiet as we both studied the picture. Then I flipped it to the back of the pile and examined the next one.

"Wow," I murmured, impressed at the artist's... er, attention to detail. "The man in the sketch really is..."

Big... well-endowed... overproportional all went through my mind, but I couldn't bring myself to utter a word.

Tuck saved me with an amused, "Yes, he is."

He made a halfhearted attempt to get the sketches back, but I turned, bumping my rear against his hip. Or maybe his groin. I wasn't sure, because those sketches gave everything a sexy spin. Like the heat of Tuck's body just behind mine. The light touch of his chest against my shoulder. The way his breath caught when my rear grazed his thigh.

I rotated the next paper right, then left, squinting.

"Wow. Is that even possible?"

Tuck chuckled. "I've never tried it."

His matter-of-fact tone suggested he'd tried quite a few moves in his time. Which really, really oughtn't have made me jealous of whoever the lucky women had been.

The dirty part of my mind stopped on that point. Women, as in, successive partners, or women, as in, several at one time?

I shook my head. Did it matter?

It shouldn't, but it did. I liked sex straight up and one-on-one. No kink, no sharing. Was Tuck the same?

I suppose I was traditional that way. Though Lord save me if anyone found out Maid Marian wasn't as innocent as they assumed.

"Are you saying you want to try?" Tuck joked.

I smacked him across the chest with the papers. Hard. And, drat the man. Why was I tempted to pat him there while I was at it?

"No, I do not want to try," I growled.

But boy, was that library getting warm. And, oops — my thoughts were drifting into sultry territory again, which I blamed on my animal side. On the other hand, that was hard to avoid, what with Tuck so comfortably close and that voice in the back of my mind.

You can trust him. You must *trust him.*

I fantasized about him slipping his arms around my waist. Leaning in slowly. Planting a kiss on my neck, then another lower. And lower...

I gulped and waved the papers in the air. "I think your friend might have missed his calling."

"Maybe he did," Tuck rumbled, moving away stiffly. "Cyril, I mean."

I turned — slowly — giving myself plenty of time to compose myself. Giving him time too, because that poke against my hip might not have been the key in his pocket.

"Here." I handed the papers over, then stepped back. "Tell Cyril his secret is safe with me."

His eyes sparkled, assuring me my secrets were safe too.

Then I caught myself. What had I been thinking, letting down my guard around him?

"Wait. Don't tell Cyril. Don't tell anyone. Do you understand?" I touched his arm. "No one can know I'm here. Please."

Every word I uttered transformed Tuck from lonely monk to bristling warrior, ready to rush off on a crusade to protect my virtue.

"No one will know." His voice was low, gravelly. Dangerous, even, as if he was ready to slay my enemies. And Lord knew I had a long list of those. One especially.

I nodded my thanks. "Good night, Tuck."

He bit his lip at the not too subtle hint. "Good night, Lady..."

I shook my head slightly. Regretfully, because part of me desperately wanted him to know who I was. What I was like. Why I was hiding in a monastery...

"Good night," I said with a tone of finality.

His lips curled in a defeated little smile, and he backed toward the door. "Good night. And while I can tell you don't need any help, just call in the unlikely event of an emergency."

Then his grin grew. "Or maybe I'll call for you when I need rescuing."

I laughed. "You do that, Friar Tuck."

He gave a little bow. "Good night, fair lady."

The door closed, and all I heard for the next few seconds were his soft footsteps on the stone stairs...and the thump of my heart, yearning.

Chapter Four

TUCK

Spiritual guidance? My ass. That woman was definitely in some kind of trouble.

Don't tell anyone you've seen me. No one can know I'm here. Please.

I lay in bed for the next few hours, thinking about it. Thinking about her.

Okay, okay — dreaming about her. I closed my eyes, picturing waves of long, glossy black hair. Eyes like two windows upon a starry night, filled with pinpoints of light. A body with curves in all the right places, but strong and agile at the same time.

Then I frowned, imagining a dozen predicaments a woman that beautiful might find herself in.

An unwanted suitor wanted her hand, and she was avoiding him.

A bad choice of lovers had come back to haunt her, and she needed to escape the fallout for a time.

An international ring of criminals was plotting to kill, kidnap, or sell her to the highest bidder.

Well, if that was the case, I pitied the criminals. They would end up rolling on the ground, clutching their balls in agony.

My lion chuckled. *Can we ask her to push us up against a wall again? Please?*

I grinned, but then my mood darkened. The fair lady keeping a low profile in the library might be more capable a fighter than most men, but even she couldn't hold off three, four, or even five attackers.

Can't let anyone harm her, my lion declared.

Still, my stomach churned at the ugly possibilities. Possibilities my mind turned over for hours in bed and all throughout Matins, the next in an endless cycle of prayers we were called to at all hours. Honestly, to God, monks must be worse than babies who refused to sleep through the night.

I yawned, then moved my lips in time to the prayers, a trick I'd learned my first week in purgatory — er, the abbey. The rare times I truly prayed, it was either to leave the abbey, for some sword-wielding barbarians to storm the abbey, or for a surprise revelation that my elder brother John — a different one, not the prince — was an impostor, thus elevating my status to second son. Then, whoopee! I would finally be a knight and could pack for the Crusades.

Sadly, none of those prayers had been answered.

Occasionally, I even prayed for world peace.

So far, that one hadn't been answered either.

However, that night — or morning, or whatever godawful hour it was — I offered up a whole new prayer. Not for myself, nor for something grand. Just for her. The captivating, intriguing, and highly armed woman in the library.

Let her be safe. Let her be happy.

That was it. Cyril had a theory that simple prayers had a better chance of slipping through all the traffic our poor Lord had to deal with, and I tended to agree.

Halfway through Matins — in other words, an eternity — I stole a glance at the abbot, then Father Benedict, his assistant and head librarian. Both were rocking in prayer — or in an attempt to remain awake, like the rest of us. Surely those two knew about the woman in the library. But why was our guest so secretive? Who was she hiding from, and why?

I kept my eyes on my book of psalms, but all I saw were her dark eyes and hair. All I smelled was her flowers-in-a-meadow scent, and all I felt was her electrifying touch on my hand...my shoulder...and, er, other places.

I shifted in my seat, fighting a hard-on. A first for me, at least in church.

Consequently, it was also the first time I didn't bolt out of my pew when prayers concluded. When I eventually joined the others filing into the cloisters, I looked up at the sky. Still dark, still mysterious. And my mind was still full of thoughts of the fair lady.

She was noble, for sure. Upper-upper-crust nobility, a good tier or two above my family. She hid her pedigree well, but it still came through in her long vowels, articulated consonants, and pauses that assumed you'd stick around to hear whatever she had to say next.

And boy, would I stick around. Not just due to her manner of speaking.

But not just due to her looks either. More like her fighting spirit. Her verve. Her determination.

We can go for walks together, my lion side enthused. *Maybe even hunting.*

Ha. Hunting was probably right up her alley. But how would she feel about heading out with, not in search of, a full-grown lion?

I think she'd love me, my lion growled, emphasizing the L-word.

I gulped, shying away from that thorny topic. Instead, I went back to dreaming — and wondering, because the mystery captivated me. What was a woman like that doing in a forgotten little abbey like this?

"I owe you," Cyril had whispered over and over once I'd handed over the sketches.

All the sketches, thank you very much, since I'd resisted the temptation to keep one for my own amusement. Because, heck. Why look at a silly sketch when my mind had the memory of the fair lady?

My breath caught there. Playing keep-away with the sketches had brought her back against my front, the way a couple would be in the slow, happy hours after lovemaking. My chin had hovered over her shoulder, and my eyes had explored the creamy skin of her neck.

And, heck. I didn't need much imagination to take things further and wake the little monk — er, big monk — in the lower half of my tunic. Even more astounding, I didn't just dwell in steamy fantasies. I spent just as much time dreaming about tamer moments. Like holding her. Walking with her. Going riding with her, side by side on a couple of easy-going horses. Even reading to her or just watching her do needlepoint.

I checked the temperature of my forehead. What was wrong with me?

And anyway, I was pretty sure the needlepoint was for show, not her real passion.

Passion, my lion rumbled, happy to fantasize a little longer.

I did my best to focus on something else. Like riding.

Wait. Riding...

My mind jumped back to the pretty white mare in the stable. The new arrival.

When the sun *finally* rose and we were *finally* released from prayers, I strode to the stable.

"Hello, Rita. Hello, Rosie." I petted both.

Rita looked at me, and I sighed. "Don't ask."

Brother Matthew had already given me an earful about my broken vow of silence, but he'd failed to assign me a new vow...yet. It was just a matter of time, I was certain.

I went over to the white mare. "Hello, you."

"Isn't she a beauty?" Geoffrey, the stableboy, said in passing.

I nodded, taking in her fine lines and noble bearing. "Beautiful *and* classy."

Geoffrey laughed. "The Maid Marian of horses, right?"

I froze.

Geoffrey went on enthusing behind me. "You should see the tack she came with. I wish my pillow was as soft as her saddle. And as for the engraving in the leather... Whoever owns her is as rich as the king. Maybe even richer."

Beautiful. Classy. Rich.

And way, way out of my league.

I glanced in the direction of the library. Maid Marian?

"Whose mount is this?" I did my best not to sound too interested.

Geoffrey shrugged. "Don't ask, because they won't tell. That's why we've got her back here with the mules. No offense, ladies," he added quickly.

Rita scuffed the ground, annoyed.

I petted the mare a moment longer, then Rita, then Rosie. Eventually, I wandered to work in the brewery, but my mind was elsewhere.

Maid Marian. Could it really be?

∞∞∞∞

I spent the whole day stealing glances at the library windows, wishing, wondering. Which made it one of the most agonizing days I'd spent at the abbey, but one of the most exciting too, because I finally had something interesting to occupy my mind.

Who was she? What was she really here for? And what were the odds of getting stabbed if I snuck into the library again that evening?

Throwing caution to the wind, I did just that, tiptoeing up the stairs an hour after lights-out in the dormitory.

Sneaking around at night had become such a regular habit that I had forgotten the adrenaline rush it used to bring. But that evening, my heart hammered and my senses piqued as I crept along. I halted at the faintest sound, the slightest hint of movement.

My inner lion twitched his whiskers. *More fun than we've had in ages.*

I grinned. And we weren't even there yet.

Around and around the stairs I went. At the rear door to the library, I paused, weighing my options. Sneaking in ran the risk of getting my throat cut by the all-too-capable woman in there. On the plus side, she might manhandle me against the wall again.

My lion hummed in approval. *Definitely worth the risk.*

It was, but how likely was she to trust me if I did?

Reluctantly, I went with option two — a light knock.

27

I held my breath, waiting.

My lion did too, picturing all kinds of nice scenarios, like her opening the door in nothing more than a bathrobe and beckoning me in.

Ten seconds later, I frowned. No answer.

I knocked again, louder. And again. And again.

Hmpf.

Of course, she was being secretive, so she was unlikely to answer the door. Or she'd left, and I would never see her again.

My lion let out a mournful growl.

Finally, I knocked as loudly as I dared, turned the key in the lock, and whispered, "I'm coming in. Please don't kill me."

I pushed the door open, then jumped back, just in case. Sure enough, the fair lady — Marian? — stood there, armed and ready.

She glared at me for a full ten seconds, then lowered her weapon — a sword this time.

"You again."

My lion mourned at her scornful tone. *She hates us.*

No, she just didn't know us yet. I still had to win her over.

She raised one perfectly curved eyebrow. "More pornographic art to retrieve?"

I shook my head. "Not tonight. And I swear, it was for a friend."

She snickered. "Right."

"It's true, but that's not why I'm here. I wanted to invite you out."

Both her eyebrows popped up.

I backtracked quickly. "I mean, not going out as in *going out*. Just literally. Go out. On a little trip to see the area. Tomorrow, I mean."

"Are you mad?"

"I know you barely know me..." I went on, undeterred.

She nodded. "You could be an assassin for all I know."

"Ha. I wish I could be something that exciting. But I promise, it will be good. You said you're here for spiritual guidance, right?"

Her chin dipped in a tiny, reluctant nod.

"Well, it's alms day tomorrow. The day we give to the poor." I paused, trying to read her expression. "It's the most meaningful activity I've found around here."

She tilted her head, and I had the uncomfortable feeling she was reading me like a book. But yes, alms day really did give me joy. And yes, my life was so empty that a once-a-week feel-good activity kept me going the other six days. That, and the hope of something more exciting from time to time, thanks to Robynne Hood. Unfortunately, her escapades didn't run on a regular schedule the way alms day did.

"Surely a lady like you knows all about giving alms," I goaded.

The nobility of our country was about a fifty-fifty split when it came to giving to the poor. Some gave more than they took; others flipped that equation. I desperately wanted Marian to belong to that first group.

"Of course." She tossed her head, looking more like a proper lady than ever. "But I don't need to come with you to do that."

A good point. I considered my options, concluding I was down to one. My joker.

I leaned in with a rough whisper. "I could take you to see Willa along the way."

And, bull's-eye. Her eyes went wide, and her breath caught. She knew Willa, all right.

A moment later, she smoothed her hands over her dress and backpedaled. "Willa who?"

Ha. Now I had her.

I tossed her the robe I'd brought.

She frowned. "What's this?"

"Your disguise."

She held it up to her body without the fuss one might expect from a highborn lady. No *I couldn't possibly be seen in something like this!* or *Don't you have something more flattering?* Just a wary look aimed at me rather than the robe.

"Hmpf. You've thought of everything, haven't you?"

I laughed. "Well, there's usually one critical detail I overlook, so brace yourself. Something is bound to go wrong."

With that, I turned for the door. "I'll pick you up in the morning, right after Terce prayers." Once at the door, I glanced back with a grin. "See you then, Marian."

Chapter Five

MARIAN

My brow furrowed as I watched Tuck prowl away. Was it that obvious who I was? Did everyone in the abbey know I was hiding in — er, visiting — the abbey?

And Willa! It would be so good to see her — if Tuck wasn't bluffing. I had a thousand questions about her too. Was she well? What was she doing? All I'd gotten was a cryptic message that said, *Delivery successful. Nosey and I safe. Staying put for the present but ready to act when you send the word.*

Questions that plagued me all night and into the next morning.

I peered out the window, wondering where Tuck was. Every time the chanting sound of monks at prayer carried through the abbey, I listened, imagining a fair-haired monk...well, maybe not praying. More like hiding under his hood and dreaming of something else.

I smiled at the image, then frowned and snatched up my needlepoint. A minute later, I threw it down again. Who was I kidding? It wasn't in my nature to play the fine lady any more than it was in Tuck's nature to live the life of a monk.

Neither was it in my nature to sit around all day. My animal side longed to get outside and run through the misty fields surrounding the abbey.

Finally, the soft pad of footsteps sounded on the back stairs. Before, that made my heart rev in alarm. Now, it revved in anticipation. But that was because of alms day, not the man I would get to spend time with. I swear.

I made sure not to answer the first soft knock, nor the second, lest he think I was overeager. Never mind that I'd spent the previous hour pacing and fiddling with my robe.

On the third knock, I opened the door with a yawn.

"Oh. It's you."

He flashed that *Here's your cue to swoon* grin and said, "Good morning."

And dammit, that rumbly tone really could make a girl swoon.

"Morning," I grumbled.

His smile grew, spreading to his cheeks and amber eyes. Then his gaze caught on the monk's robe I wore, and his breath caught.

I frowned, looking down. "Did I do it wrong?"

He shook his head quickly. "On the contrary. All good. *Too* good." Then he cleared his throat and reached for my rope belt. "May I?"

I kept my arms out of the way, pretending not to enjoy him rearranging the belt.

Then he cleared his throat again, backed away, and took in his handiwork.

"Good. Right. Perfect. Except the hair, maybe. I mean, it is perfect, but that's not the point. I mean..."

Aha. So, it was possible to get this smooth operator flustered. Good to know.

I brushed my hair back and flipped the hood up. "Better?"

"Better." His voice was a little wobbly, though.

I followed him down the back stairs and out a side door. And boy, when it came to stealthy, the man was a pro.

Lion shifter, my beast side murmured dreamily.

I knew a few, and while Tuck had the same fighting spirit, he was different too. More playful, less snobby. Unique, in a word.

My animal side grinned. *We're a perfect match.*

I sighed. If only things were that simple.

He paused to peek around every corner, reminding me of the spy games Willa and I had played as children. My spirits soared at the chance to see her.

Still, I'd packed brass knuckles and several daggers, just in case the good friar wasn't as sunny or honest as he seemed.

"Link your hands at your stomach, keep your chin down, and stay beside me," he instructed when we stepped outside.

My breath crystallized before me, and my worn riding boots crunched over the frosty ground. I was sure someone would see through my cover, but the few monks we passed gave uninterested nods in passing.

Inside the stable, Tuck worked briskly to hitch two mules to a wagon.

"Come now, Rita," he murmured, backing one into position.

Ah, lucky girl, to feel those big, capable hands moving over her body and hear her name murmured from so close.

I coughed a little and petted my horse, who perked her ears excitedly.

"Sorry, Snow. Not today."

I petted Rita next, and she swished her tail contentedly. Then I caught Tuck studying me.

"What?" I demanded.

He rubbed his chin. "The girls are cranky around anyone but Geoffrey or me." He glanced down the row of stalls extending along the barn, and though he didn't say it, his expression said, *Some of the other horses too.*

I flashed a smile, though it was a little forced. "I guess I have a way with horses, and my father always said I'm as stubborn as a mule."

I kept my eyes down, lest he see through me. It wasn't a lie, but it wasn't entirely the truth either.

The wagon was already loaded with sacks of bread, potatoes, and other such goods. Something clinked when Tuck concealed a lumpy pouch among them. Coins?

Tuck broke into a coughing fit, then flashed an innocent smile. "Well, we must get going. Need a hand, m'lady?"

I sprang up and took the reins. "Got it all under control, thank you."

"I can see that." He took the spot beside me on the driver's bench, then spread a blanket across our legs. "For the cold," he added quickly.

Too quickly. So maybe I wasn't the only one entertaining images of snuggling intimately under a shared blanket.

"Of course," I said dryly.

He clicked to the mules, and the wagon lurched into motion.

"That way, fair lady." He pointed once we were outside.

"Don't call me fair lady."

"Give me a name, then."

I kept my lips sealed.

"How about Marian?" he proposed.

I gulped. I'd hoped his comment the previous evening had been a wild guess, but it seemed he really did have me figured out. Drat. I shot him a hard look and played my ace.

"You can call me Marian if I can call you...say, Leo."

His jaw dropped, and his lips moved a little. I could practically see the gears move in his mind. *She knows I'm a lion shifter?*

Then he flared his nostrils, testing my scent. And testing and testing...

"Wolf?" he finally murmured.

I shook my head.

"Fox?"

I snorted. I was no canine.

He looked perplexed. "Lion? Dragon? Bear?"

My smile grew smug. "None of those things."

I probably shouldn't have revealed I wasn't entirely human, but it had just slipped out, and I doubted he would ever guess.

His voice dropped ominously on his next try. "Witch?"

"God, no."

For the next long minute, the only sound was that of the mules and the creaking wagon. Then he tried again.

"Hedgehog?"

I smacked him. "Hedgehog?"

He laughed. "Okay, maybe not a hedgehog. What, then?"

I didn't say a word.

Finally, he gave in. "A woman of many secrets, I see. All right, I give up. For now." Twisting in his seat, he produced a couple of hot cross buns and a flask. "Warm cider. We've got a long day ahead of us."

We did, and it was, though I enjoyed every minute. Despite the chill of winter and the fallow fields all around, there was a subtle beauty to the landscape.

"Oh! Look!" I pointed at a doe and her leggy fawn, surrounded by mist by the side of a stream.

"Very pretty. Oh!" He looked at me closely. "Deer shifter?"

I laughed and shook my head, then went back to watching the doe and her fawn. We both marveled at the beauty of that wintery scene, then looked at each other and grinned.

And grinned. . .

Slowly, our smiles faded, but not because something was wrong. On the contrary, something was very, very right. His amber eyes locked on mine, sparking and swirling. My chest rose on a deep breath, and time slowed.

The wagon wheels rumbled over frozen ground, and my mind turned the sound into words.

Trust. . . destiny. . . love. . .

All concepts I thought I understood, except I hadn't, at least not until now.

Which was crazy. I barely knew the man!

You can trust him. You must trust him, the wheels creaked to me next.

Can trust was one thing. But *must*? Why? What did fate have in store?

Rosie nickered, and we both looked up. Another wagon was coming our way.

Tuck gave himself a little shake. "Whoops. We've got company." He smoothed a hand over my head, hiding a loose lock of hair, and tugged my hood lower. "Keep your head down."

I did, hiding my face as the other wagon rolled by.

"Morning, Tuck," someone called.

"Morning, Anthony," Tuck echoed.

"Who was that?" I whispered once we were clear.

"The lay monk on firewood duty."

For a while, neither of us spoke. Then I leaned in and whispered, "What about Willa?"

He pointed, and at first, I didn't understand. No house, no village. Just a seemingly endless stretch of woods.

Then it hit me. The woods.

"She's in Sherwood Forest?"

Tuck kept his lips pursed as if weighing up how much to trust me.

"Can we see her now? Is that where we're going?"

He shook his head. "You don't enter the forest without an invitation — not even me. But I've sent word. She knows my route. So, it's up to her."

Heat rose to my cheeks, and I nearly barked an angry reply. But then I caught myself. Tuck was simply protecting my friend — and himself.

I sat back, resolving to let the day bring what it would — such as evidence that I could trust Tuck, and vice versa. And hopefully, a chance to see Willa.

My mind went over his words. *You don't enter the forest without an invitation. Not even me.*

Did he know the outlaws of Sherwood Forest? Did he have some kind of agreement with them?

I glanced at the goods in the wagon, worried that I'd misjudged Tuck. What if he planned to sell the goods intended for the poor and pocket the profits? Worse, what if he was in cahoots with the bandits?

Months earlier, I'd sent Willa — my best friend and, technically, one of my ladies-in-waiting — on a secret mission to bring my family treasures to the outlaws of Sherwood Forest for safekeeping from Prince John. But what if my trust in them had been misplaced?

I studied Tuck closely. "You're not worried about bandits?"

He laughed. "I would love some action to spice up my day. But sadly, the local gangs disagree." When I cocked my head, he explained. "They tried robbing me once. I went easy on them, but unfortunately, they've refused to come out and play ever since."

That was all too easy to picture — Tuck as a warrior, fighting a half-dozen robbers.

"Besides, the new sheriff — acting sheriff, I mean — has chased away most of the bandits," he continued. "The man's too damn efficient for his own good."

I motioned toward the forest. "What about Robin Hood and the Merry Men?"

He smirked. "Now, that's an entirely different breed of bandit. They don't bother honest folk. Quite the opposite, in fact."

I crooked an eyebrow, waiting.

He laughed. "All right, all right. They don't mess with *poor* folks. Rich folks, on the other hand, are fair game."

"Because. . . ?"

He narrowed his eyes at me, then whispered, "Because they serve the poor in the name of our true king, Richard. You'll see."

I certainly hoped so.

The only sounds for the next twenty minutes were the creak of the wagon and the quiet thud of the mules' hooves. Then we stopped at a tiny hamlet, not more than four or five households.

"Friar Tuck! Friar Tuck!" People who had peered out warily smiled upon recognizing him. "Welcome!"

"Hello, George. Hello, Maud. Hello, Jamie."

Greeting each by name, Tuck got to work immediately, distributing food, clothing, and other goods.

"I've got bread, potatoes, and everyone's favorite — turnips," he joked.

All were eagerly accepted, along with profuse thanks.

"Here's that new axe blade you needed," he told one man. "And a bolt of cloth for you and the children," he said, presenting it to a woman with a flourish. "Plus tea and salt for you, Miss Maggie." That was a woman so old and stooped, she could barely walk with a cane, yet she came alive at Tuck's doting attention.

"You must stay for tea," she insisted.

He winked. "I'd love to, but won't the neighbors talk?"

Her cheeks went all rosy as she took his elbow. "Let them."

He laughed heartily, and the sound livened up the whole dreary community.

Like so many other places in the land, the hamlet showed signs of long-gone prosperity — peeling paint, crooked rooflines. Proud, simple folks in patched, worn clothing. Mothers whose eyes shone with love for their children but filled with despair when talk turned to the future.

Over the years of the king's absence, Prince John had raised taxes higher and higher. But there was only so much blood to be squeezed from a turnip, as the saying went. I doubted these people had ever been rich, but now, they teetered on the edge of survival.

Tuck introduced me as Brother Michael. "One of our newest novices. He's taken a vow of silence, so please don't tempt him."

Clever man, that Tuck.

I watched, fascinated, as he made his rounds. He drank tea and made conversation. He helped haul slate shingles to a rooftop in desperate need of repair. He admired babies and played knight with the children. That meant jousting with sticks, playing good guy *and* bad guy, and allowing himself to be tackled by a dozen laughing youngsters.

I couldn't help picturing a father lion covered in playful cubs, making sure to be gentle while pretending to be fierce.

"Help! Help me, fair maiden!" he called to Maggie.

The older woman giggled. "No one's called me that in decades."

Eventually, Tuck shook the children off — carefully — and made his goodbyes. "I'd love to stay, but duty calls. Besides, your knights terrify me."

Everyone mourned at our departure, and when we looked back from a rise half a mile down the road, they were still waving. Tuck waved back, and whatever part of me hadn't yet melted gave up resisting.

"You're good at that," I murmured.

He chuckled. "Playing with kids? My mother says it's because I still haven't grown up."

I pinned him with a sharp look. "You do more than that. You treat people with respect. You give them a sense of dignity."

He stared at me, taken aback. His lips parted, and I sensed a self-deprecating joke coming, but then they closed again. A moment later, he shrugged. "I try."

"You succeed," I assured him.

His manners, speech, and the fact that he could read suggested he came from a noble family. But he really had a heart for people — all people, no matter their age, class, or circumstances.

"I think you were born for this job," I declared as the mules plodded faithfully toward our next stop.

He heaved an exaggerated sigh. "Here I was, thinking I was born to be a knight."

I shook my head. "You were born for greater things."

He eyed me skeptically, as if to say, *There's something greater than knighthood?*

Yes, there was. He might not know it yet, but maybe someday, he would come to that realization.

"You're already leaving your mark on the world — in a good way. How many knights can say the same?"

He looked at me, uncharacteristically quiet for a while.

"What about you?" he finally asked.

I tilted my head. "What about me?"

"What were you born for?"

I snorted. "Don't you know? To marry well and bear many babies."

Lord, save me, I nearly added.

He shook his head. "That's what you're expected to do. But what were you born for?"

A man after my own heart.

"As a child, I planned to be a knight," I admitted. "Suffice to say, that job wasn't open to me."

Tuck laughed. "Now, there's something I can relate to."

Perhaps, but I was the only daughter of a widowed nobleman, and duty was an invisible corset that restricted my movements. Not to mention the greatest duty of all — keeping my family's deepest secret.

There'd been many times I'd nearly shared it with Willa, my best friend and confidante. Now, I was just as tempted to confide in Tuck. But I couldn't. I wasn't allowed to tell anyone.

Tuck leaned in close enough to bump my shoulder. "Well, I think you're born for great things. Whatever they are."

I sighed. "Like getting married and doing needlepoint for the rest of my life?"

He nodded solemnly. "Greater even than needlepoint."

We laughed, and when our eyes met, so much passed between us, I forgot where I was. I forgot *who* I was and why I was even there. All I registered was the glow of his eyes and the crackling energy that filled the air around us.

His eyes dropped to my mouth, and my lips twitched. But the wagon lurched just then, and the reins jerked in my hands.

I sat upright, looking ahead. Oops.

Tuck murmured, pointing, "That way. Lunchtime stop. Bess's place."

Bess, as it turned out, was a widowed mother of three — and she was younger than me. Her croft was tiny, with a rickety barn and a handkerchief of a garden. But somehow, she got by on that and a modest income from a small herd of sheep.

Her expression was tired and wary until she recognized Tuck. Then she broke into a huge smile that let her beauty shine through.

"Friar Tuck!"

He doffed an imaginary cap. "Lady Bess."

She blushed.

The children ran up, calling, "Tuck! Tuck!"

Our visit echoed the previous stops. Tuck played with the children while I helped Bess with lunch. It was all so relaxed, so familiar. Then we all sat and enjoyed the feast Tuck had brought. I leaned back, shocked at how desperately the children attacked the meal. My heart went out to them as I took in their patched clothes and thin shoulders.

Prince John might not be to blame for this young woman's difficult life, but I cursed him anyway, along with the rest of the world. Why did a lucky few have so much, while others had so little?

"Delicious," Bess murmured between bites.

Now I knew why Tuck had brought enough for several feasts — enough to keep the family going for a while. But even if he'd come empty-handed, I was sure he would get an equally warm welcome, thanks to his energy and good cheer.

"Can I go live with Tuck?" Tom, the eldest, asked.

Bess smiled. "When you grow up, you can join the clergy, like him."

Tuck choked, and I thumped his back.

"Maybe you should keep your options open," Tuck advised.

"My father was a stone mason," Tom said proudly.

"Well, maybe we can find you an apprenticeship when the time comes," Tuck said.

"Do stone masons have a lot to eat?" Tom asked.

Bess sighed. "When they have work."

My heart wept, and I slid a ring from my finger. As a present from my father, it was dear to me, but its sale price could feed the family for a month.

Tuck covered my hand with his and tilted his head toward the goods he'd placed in the kitchen. Then he stood, pulling me with him.

"Well, this has been lovely, but we must go. Make sure you unpack those things I brought and keep them safe."

A smile dawned on my lips as I remembered the pouch of coins. He'd left some for Bess along with other supplies, hadn't he?

"I will," Bess promised. "Thank you so much."

"My pleasure. And you, big man. Take care of this family."

Tom nodded earnestly. "Yes, sir."

We left with hugs and promises to return soon. It was only half a mile down the road when I realized that only applied to Tuck. I was just passing through here.

Somehow, the thought made me ache.

"Good people," I whispered as the mules plodded on.

"Good, indeed," Tuck murmured, just as thoughtful as I was.

For the next minute, contemplative silence reigned.

Then Tuck cleared his throat. "Now, about Willa—"

I nodded eagerly, but he stopped, whipping his head around. When I followed his gaze, my blood froze.

A cloud of dust rose from a dozen galloping horses along a road — one of many converging on Nottingham, another mile away. The riders' armor glinted, as did their spears and swords. A fine carriage brought up the rear, pulled by four coal-black horses.

Tuck cursed, studying the flag flapping over it.

The curtain at the carriage window moved, and instinct made me tug down my hood. A hand appeared next, and my breath caught. The grim reaper didn't travel with such fanfare, but I swore, I sensed death and evil. So much, I felt the urge to flee. Even the mules panicked, pulling in opposite directions.

"Whoa there," I called, pulling myself together. I didn't have to stand by and surrender to that sense of fear. I closed my eyes, reaching out with my thoughts.

A moment later, the mules settled down. But as for the carriage in the distance...

One of the horses stumbled, and the whole carriage lurched. The hand at the window disappeared as the passenger was thrown back. The driver hung on for dear life as they careened along on the verge of stampeding.

"Whoa," Tuck murmured. Then he glanced at me.

I kept a straight face. "Nice carriage, but it smells of trouble."

He studied me a moment longer, then nodded grimly. "It does. That's the Gisborne family flag."

Word of Sir Guy's death had traveled quickly through the land, and I, like most, had celebrated. But that didn't mean the danger was past. Not with his sister still on the prowl.

"Lady Thornton," I murmured darkly.

Tuck nodded. "Headed to Nottingham. We have to put off that rendezvous with Willa."

Disappointment ran deep, but I suspected that was the least of my worries.

Tuck clucked to the mules, and they picked up their pace immediately.

"We're not heading to Nottingham?" I asked.

He shook his head grimly. "We have to get back to the abbey — and get a message to Sherwood Forest. As soon as possible."

Chapter Six

TUCK

That evening, I was still daydreaming about it all — er, I mean, deeply engrossed in Bible-study hour — when Brother Matthew snapped his fingers and whispered, "You're wanted in the abbot's office."

I blinked a few times, then stood and strode for the door.

Twenty sympathetic pairs of eyes followed me, communicating something like, *Good luck, man. You'll need it.*

Cyril gave me a tight smile.

For summons by the abbot, I usually called on my vast experience getting into trouble back in my school days. But today, I slipped my hands into the single front pocket of my robe — the second-best feature of the garb, after the hood — and rubbed them nervously. Had the abbot caught wind of my visits to the library? Worse, would I get Marian in trouble?

Father Benedict, the abbot's assistant and head librarian, was inscrutable, as usual. He made me sit outside the abbot's office for a good thirty minutes... as usual. Finally, at no discernible signal, he sighed and motioned me forward. After one solemn knock on the door, he opened it, shooed me in, then backed away, closing it.

"Good morning," I murmured, taking a seat before the abbot.

Totally not protocol, because you were supposed to stand quietly until otherwise instructed, as I'd learned the hard way on my first visit, a mere three hours after entering the monastery. A new record, apparently. And all I'd done was ask how much longer prayers would take.

How little I'd known back then, because the answer was, prayers never ended. They merely allowed mini breaks for us to sneak in a little work, sleep, or food. Then it was right back to the never-ending cycle.

The abbot looked at me. I looked back.

I persisted in breaking protocol in vague hopes of someday getting expelled, though I'd never gone as far as putting my feet on his desk.

"Friar Tuck," he began at his usual slow pace.

I resisted the urge to stir the air with my hands.

"You'll be taking your vows soon."

His pauses were hard to identify, given the ponderous manner of his speech, but as the silence stretched, I decided it was a pause, indeed.

I gritted my teeth, waiting. He didn't expect me to cry, *Yippee!* and throw my hands in the air, did he?

"Father Benjamin and I have met and discussed your case..." he went on.

I held back a snort. Cyril, I was sure, did not have a case. Neither did Bartholomew or any of the other novices. But my file was probably as thick as the biggest volumes in the library.

The library, my lion sighed, thinking of Marian.

"It seems you have had difficulties adjusting in the six months you have been here..." he said.

I nearly burst out laughing at the understatement.

"...which naturally leads us to question your prospects of ever doing so."

Nil, I nearly cut in. *The prospects are nil. I will never, ever adjust to this life, no matter how long I might live.*

My lion mourned. *To think, we could have spent our time with Marian.*

That was new. Normally, the thought was more along the lines of, *We could have spent our time as a knight.*

That too, my lion threw in, but only as an afterthought.

I looked at the abbot. It killed me to think of someday being as old and gray as him with nothing to show for it but a hell of a lot of prayers. Not that I had anything against prayers — just the sheer volume of them.

"Therefore, we have come to a decision," he announced.

Sweat broke out on my brow. What if he transferred me to another monastery — somewhere far from Sherwood Forest and, worse, from Marian?

"Much as it pains us — and much as it will no doubt pain your family — we have decided to remove you from the path you have set upon."

I frowned. What exactly did that mean? A path of sin? If so, which one?

He motioned to the door. "Go, my son. May God have mercy on your soul."

I peeked in case an executioner stood by the door. Was I being sent to the gallows?

"Go on, then," he chided me. "Shoo."

Shoo?

I looked at the door, then back at him. "Go...where?"

He motioned again, irritated. "Just go. You are free. We relieve you of the duties you are so ill-suited for."

I dreaded the worst. "And what duties would you assign me instead?"

"None. We release you from the abbey. You are no longer bound to this life."

My heart leaped. He was releasing me from the clergy?

I frowned. Wait. Was this some kind of trick?

I studied him, waiting for the punch line. And waiting...and waiting...

I scratched my head. Surely he had a hidden motive.

Doesn't matter. Run for freedom while you can, my lion urged.

Every muscle in my body strained to do exactly that. But something held me back.

"Why?" I asked.

The abbot threw up his hands, exasperated. "You have neither the temperament nor the constitution to be a man of God."

True, but that had been obvious from day one. It wasn't as if they'd only figured that out now.

"Further, you are a bad influence on the other candidates."

Also true, if *bad* meant trying to get them to see the light — or maybe *not* to see the light, I supposed.

He motioned to the door. "As I said, you are free to go."

Now, his tapping foot added.

It ought to have been the best day of my life, but somehow, I couldn't move. Was this sheer luck, or were evil forces behind this somehow?

Lady Thornton, my lion growled.

She was evil, all right, but I couldn't imagine how her arrival in Nottingham connected to me.

Then I considered Marian. Had someone discovered my visits to the library?

"Of course, once you depart, you are forbidden from ever returning," the abbot threw in.

Hardly a punishment — except in terms of Marian. If I left now, how would I see her? How could I protect her? Clearly, she was in some kind of trouble, even danger — danger amplified now that Lady Thornton was around. So, staying in the abbey was my best means of remaining close to Marian.

A double-edged sword, because when she moved on, I would still be stuck here. Forever. No use to her, no use to myself, and definitely no use to the church.

There was only one thing to do. Stall.

"Thank you, sir. I'll think about it." I turned for the door quickly.

"Friar Tuck," he barked.

I halted, slowly turning back.

"This is a one-time offer. If you reject it now — and I cannot fathom why you might — it will never be open to you again. You will take your vows as planned and become a member of the clergy for life."

I gulped. My life — my whole life — was on the line. But wasn't Marian's, potentially?

"Think about it, Tuck," the abbot warned.

I was thinking about it, dammit. It was deciding that was hard.

"Poverty, obedience, chastity." The abbot put extra emphasis on the last word.

Boy, did he know how to build a case.

And maybe he was right. As a normal citizen, I could follow Marian if she left the abbey. But a man expelled from the clergy was a man without honor. Even if Marian tolerated my presence, others wouldn't. I couldn't just waltz into the next castle she sought refuge in on the basis of *pretty please.*

Besides, quitting the clergy would put a stain on my family's good name forever. My parents had little enough to be proud of in me. They would be aghast at a failure of this magnitude.

My stomach churned at the thought of the fallout — for everyone, not just myself.

Briefly, I considered faking a new identity and heading to the Crusades. But the best I could hope for was work as a foot soldier or a knight's page, which were about as close to my dream as becoming town crier of Nottingham. There just wasn't the same appeal.

Of course, I could join the Merry Men. But that wouldn't help Marian, and it wouldn't help Robynne. On the contrary, it was critical for her to have someone on the inside.

Someone like me.

The lump in my throat doubled in size.

"Tuck..." the abbot started softly. Clearly, he was transitioning to the *good cop* role. "Ever since the day you arrived, you've wanted to leave."

My shoulders sagged. True.

But Marian had changed everything. So had Robynne, albeit in a different way. Two strong women, determined to take charge of their own fates. Surely I should do the same?

But it wasn't the same, because their actions served the greater good. Mine would only profit myself and let down everyone else.

As the abbot went on, I barely heard his words. All I heard was my lion grumbling inside, together with a deeper, ephemeral voice.

Your fate lies here, it assured me.

If only this were a physical fight! I would know what weapon to wield and where to place every blow. But making a decision like this was a nightmare confined to my head. No commands to obey, no enemy to slay. Just a crossroads and beyond that, nothing but mist and mysteries.

Your fate lies here, the voice insisted.

I looked outside, taking in the fields, the river, and the distant forest. Then I looked at the library window, where a shadow moved. Marian?

I swallowed hard, because I knew what I had to do. I knew I would hate it, too. But a true knight was a man of honor.

"Thank you, Father."

He brightened. "You have decided."

I forced myself to nod. "Yes. Now, I must go."

He practically rubbed his hands in glee. "Indeed, you must. Gather your things, say your goodbyes..."

I shook my head. "I must go study. After all, I take my vows in less than a week."

The abbot's jaw dropped, and the church bells chose exactly then to sound a solemn *bong, bong, bong.*

Chapter Seven

MARIAN

It had been a long day full of impressions. Unfortunately, the one I kept coming back to was Lady Thornton's arrival in Nottingham. It didn't seem fair that she overshadowed more pleasant memories of Tuck's good deeds.

I flopped down on the library's daybed, staring into the distance. What was Lady Thornton doing in Nottingham? Whatever it was, her visit spelled trouble.

A light knock sounded at the main door, and I waited. A moment later came a double knock — the arranged signal, which I echoed. A moment later, a third knock sounded, and I unlocked the door, then stepped back.

With a creak, it swung open, and Father Benedict entered with a tray of food. He and the abbot were the only two souls in the abbey who knew of my visit.

And now Tuck too, my second side hummed happily.

Thank goodness for that. He was much better company.

"Good evening, miss," Father Benedict murmured.

I nodded, making space on the table. "Good evening."

He looked at the books I moved aside, nodding at one in approval. "Ah, one of our newest titles. Hildegard of Bingen's *Physica*. A most appropriate choice."

Ha. I'd placed it there exactly for that purpose. Every time the man entered, I had the feeling he was alert for every detail. *Physica* was a medical tome — one of the few topics deemed appropriate for a noble lady such as myself.

Next, he held up Peter Lombard's *The Sentences - Book 2*, an exceedingly dull treatise on God's reasons for creation, among other heady topics.

"I'm on *Distinctions 12–15*," I bluffed. "Fascinating."

Not really, but it suited my purpose.

"Excellent choice, miss. Excellent choice," Benedict hummed.

A good thing he didn't notice the volume I'd hidden under the table: *Deeds of the Franks and the other pilgrims to Jerusalem*, a memoir of the First Crusade. I'd been saving it for Tuck's next visit.

Benedict lifted a ceramic cover, revealing a steaming plate of potatoes and a slice of ham.

"We eat quite simply here, I'm afraid."

He said that every day, even when the meals weren't as simple as I'd assumed a monastery's would be. I made a mental note to ask Tuck what he'd been served. Was I getting special treatment, or was this an indication of how Benedict ate?

"It's perfect, thank you."

I stood stiffly by the table as he moved around the library, snooping. His eyes fell on my bag... my needlepoint... the bed... my boots...

I tensed as he inspected them. A good thing I'd cleaned them after my outing.

"I hope the potatoes are cooked to your liking," he murmured.

I couldn't have cared less, but it seemed polite to sample them before answering. I sat, took a bite, then said, "Delicious. Thank you."

Something rasped, and I turned just in time to see Benedict shove something into his pocket. He flashed a fake grin and hurried to the main door.

"Enjoy your meal," he called, stepping outside before I could react.

For a moment, I sat rooted in place, suspicious, though not sure of what exactly. Then I ran to the door — too late. The lock turned from the other side.

I shoved the door hard, but it didn't budge. Then I slid open the peephole cover.

"What is the meaning of this?" I demanded.

Benedict smirked. "For your own protection, dear lady."

A good thing for him that peephole wasn't big enough for my fist.

"I'm a guest here, not a prisoner!"

God, I could have clawed his eyeballs out in that moment.

"Indeed, you are a guest. And we take our guests' safety very seriously."

"I demand to see the abbot. You have no right!"

"We are here to do the Lord's work, I assure you, miss." The key disappeared into his robes, and he placed his palms together in a manner of prayer. "Good evening."

With that, he padded down the stairs.

I could have screamed in frustration, but I didn't want to give him the satisfaction. Instead, I slammed the peephole shut and backed away.

Fine. There was still the rear door. I ran over, then cursed. That must have been the key I'd seen him pocket, because it was gone, and the door was locked. On the other side was the spare key Tuck used, but I couldn't reach it. I checked the windows next, but it was a long, long way down to the ground. The library took up the building's third story, but high ceilings made it more like four or five stories.

A whinny sounded from across the way — Snow, in the barn, sensing my panic. Moments later, the other horses joined in, whinnying and kicking in their stalls. The red glow of sunset bathed the monks who ran to see what was amiss. Was Tuck among them?

I backed away from the windows, forcing myself to exude calm. If Snow and the other horses kept up that ruckus, they were bound to hurt themselves.

I'm all right, I willed them to hear. *Everything is all right.*

But, mistress, they cried back. All of them, not just Snow. *What has threatened you?*

Horses didn't talk so much as listen — and boy, did they listen. That made them highly attuned to emotions, especially when it came to members of the noblest family lines, like me. But our numbers were dwindling, and our unique heritage was our deepest, most precious secret.

Everything is all right, I assured the distraught equines. *I'm sorry to have alarmed you.*

Slowly, I sensed them settling down — all except Snow, who knew me best.

Mistress, she called, still on edge. *What is it?*

A complication, I admitted, though only to her. *But I can handle it. If I need help, I'll alert you.*

Snow, like me, had been trained for various emergency scenarios. If she had to kick her way out of her stall, she could do it. But a horse wouldn't be much help in obtaining a key and turning a lock, only for a quick getaway after I broke out of the library.

I took a deep breath, considering how soon I might need that quick getaway.

It's all right, Snow. Be still now. But be ready.

She nickered in my mind, then faded to the background as I considered my situation.

I'd come to Winslow Abbey because the abbot was a staunch supporter of King Richard and, thus, of my family. But I hadn't been counting on the likes of Father Benedict. Was he allied with Prince John? Or was he a man of no particular conviction, ready to sell me to the highest bidder?

Either way, it hardly mattered. I checked the weapons concealed among my garments and placed my sword beside the door. Then I took my extra weapons from my bag and distributed them in strategic places. I even placed the long needle of my project in such a way as to make it easy to grab in case of emergency. The next time Benedict — or anyone else — appeared at the door, I would be ready.

Until then, I paced, wondering, worrying.

∞∞∞∞∞

Night fell. The monks were called to evening prayer. When they finished and filed out again, the abbey settled into its normal nighttime silence.

Silent but for my footfalls, padding back and forth across the length of the library.

An hour later, I halted in my tracks, hearing a different set of footfalls on the rear stairway. I drew my longest dagger and stood, waiting.

Metal scraped. The lock turned. The door creaked open. Beyond it, darkness.

"Marian?" someone whispered.

Relief washed over me, and I dropped my defenses. "Tuck!"

He stepped cautiously into sight — smart man, given our first encounter — and I nearly launched myself into his arms.

And, oops. I did launch myself into a tight hug. For a moment, he stood there, surprised. Then he slowly wrapped his arms around me and hugged back.

"Good to see you too," he murmured.

If I hadn't been so busy holding him, I might have laughed out loud. King Richard could have shown up at my door, and I wouldn't have been as relieved.

I took a deep breath, calming myself. Or maybe that was Tuck doing the calming. Because, wow. His arms were corded with muscle, his chest a hard plate of armor. But his voice, like his touch, was gentle.

"Everything all right?"

I straightened my dress awkwardly as he put the spare key back in its spot. "Yes. No. Possibly..."

He cocked his head, waiting the way Snow did. Patiently. Loyally. As if my wish was his command and he was ready to jump into action.

I motioned to the main door. "What do you think of Father Benedict?"

He frowned. "He's strict. No sense of humor. Prays a lot. Like everyone else here, I suppose."

I snorted. "Well, he's the first to lock me up in here."

Tuck's eyes went wide. "What?"

I told him about the whole *blink and you'll miss it* encounter.

"He took both keys — front and rear doors. Now I'm really locked in."

Tuck's eyes went dangerously dark, and when he muttered Benedict's name, the stubble on his chin thickened — his lion side prowling toward the surface.

"Why would he do that?"

I pursed my lips. So far, I'd been careful not to tell Tuck much. But it was time to come clean — at least, with a few basics. My deepest family secrets, I would never reveal.

"Because there's a price on my head."

He blinked. "Like Robin Hood?"

I laughed. "Nothing that exciting, unfortunately. Prince John is after me, but for entirely different reasons."

"Reasons like. . . ?"

I made a face. "I'm Marian, only daughter of Lord Newton, loyal follower of King Richard."

"So, Prince John wants to eliminate a potential enemy," Tuck surmised.

I laughed. Ah, to be a man and think only of such trivial matters.

"He wants more. He wants *me*."

Tuck stared a moment, then clenched and unclenched his fists.

"He wants. . ." He didn't finish the sentence, but he did glance at the bed.

The reminder sickened me, but it was nice to see Tuck outraged. Most folks just shrugged and counseled me to accept my fate. As a woman, I was merely an asset to be traded or discarded. Enlightened men like my father were a minority, and I feared it would take decades for our backward society to change.

But, hell. I planned to do my best to speed things forward.

"Prince John has asked for — no, demanded — my hand in marriage. I have until the feast of Saint Matthias to marry him."

Tuck scratched his jaw. "Saint Matthias, patron saint of carpenters, tailors, and smallpox victims?" Then he blinked in surprise. "Wow. I've actually learned something here."

"What else about Saint Matthias?" I prompted.

Tuck shot me an annoyed look. "Boy, you're as bad as Father Benjamin, who leads the novices' lessons."

Given my current situation, my sympathy had its bounds, so I jumped to the answer. "Saint Matthias replaced Judas as Christ's twelfth apostle."

Tuck still looked blank. I wanted to shake him.

"Don't you see? Matthias replaced Judas..."

Tuck's eyes lit in realization. "And Prince John wants to replace King Richard."

"Exactly. I fear he plans to marry me and claim the throne for himself, using my family name to underscore his power."

Tuck's teeth extended in a sign of lion rage. "When is the feast of Saint Matthias?"

"February 24."

Tuck's jaw dropped. "But that's...that's..."

I nodded wearily. "Next week. That's why I came here."

He looked skeptical. "I hate to say it, but missing the date won't make Prince John look for a better prospect." He snorted to himself. "Not that he'd find one. Where else is he going to find someone so rich, beautiful, and politically useful?"

I smacked him. "Thank you?"

He stuck up his hands. "I'm thinking the way he would think, not how I think. Although you are beautiful." He fended off my next smack. "Just saying! It's not what I value in you."

I stuck a hand on my hip. "No? What do you value in me, then?"

He shrugged. "Everything. You're kind. You care. You're classy, but not snobby."

I snorted. "And you know this because...?"

"I saw all that yesterday. Also, you know weapons. Definitely a plus point."

My lips curled up.

"Your needlepointing leaves something to be desired..." he went on, waving at the canvas.

I huffed. "That's your measure of character?"

"No. That's the point. You're not content to do what you're supposed to do. You get out and do important things. *Really* important things."

My lips cracked open, but no words came out, because what exactly did you say to something like that? *Thank you? You're the only man who's ever bothered to see beyond the obvious?*

For a moment, we stared at each other. My arms twitched with the urge to hug him. Warmth filled the chilly space between us, and I swear, my eyes glowed the way Tuck's did.

Then Tuck gave himself a little shake and pulled me toward the back stairs.

"We can discuss details later. Right now, you have to get out of here."

I followed him gladly, winding down the dark spiral staircase. But gradually, my steps slowed.

"Wait."

"Wait?" Tuck echoed, exasperated. "We have to get you out of here. Prince John could be on his way now."

I held my ground, struggling to put my spinning mind in order. "What if... What if I stayed?"

Tuck stared. "Are you crazy?"

I shook my head. "Think about it. Father Benedict thinks he has me trapped. That gives me a certain advantage."

Tuck looked like he wanted to shake me. "Advantage, how?"

"It will take the urgency off his rush to contact the prince, and in the same way, the prince will think he doesn't have to hurry to get me. He has until next week."

Tuck gaped. "How close do you dare cut this exactly?"

I shrugged. "The longer I wait, the more time I buy. Just consider... Prince John's enemies — and there are many— are my allies. And I haven't spent the last months idly. I've been visiting my family's closest associates, building a network..."

Tuck listened intently. "How big a network?"

"Big. So far, they've been hoping for King Richard to return and take care of Prince John himself. So, I haven't been able to get them to commit to making a move. But if they see Prince John preparing to make his own power play..."

"Like a wedding," Tuck mused. "The perfect place to make a grand announcement..."

I nodded. "February 24. A few days away."

Tuck rubbed a hand over his jaw. "I see your point, but..."

I took his hands. "There is no *but*. Making myself a sitting duck will embolden the prince to make his move — a move that will be obvious to everyone. So obvious, my allies will act quickly."

Tuck shook his head. "Too much can go wrong."

I snorted. "Is that what knights say on the eve of battle?"

He looked at his feet. "I suppose not."

I poked him. "So what do they do?"

He studied me, then stared into the darkness. "They plan. Gather intelligence. They prepare to live or die for their principles."

I nodded grimly. "And then they launch their attack. Exactly as we will."

He looked surprised — and honored. "We?"

I flashed a warm smile. "You, me... and hopefully, a hell of a lot of backup."

He laughed softly, then cupped my cheek, going all serious. "You, Maid Marian, would make a fine general."

I chuckled. "And you, Friar Tuck, would make a fine knight." I let a beat go by, then smiled. "A kiss for good luck?"

He broke into a huge grin. "Well, seeing as you're the general..."

"True," I murmured, inching closer. "And since orders are orders..."

A beam of moonlight separated us, but I cut through it, pressing my body against his. Then I leaned up and forward, touching my lips to his. Wrapping my arms around him, too, and squeezing hard enough to erase any space between us. The kiss went deeper and deeper, hungrier and hungrier, until my whole body burned for his. I squeezed my hips closer and my arms lower...

A loud flutter sounded, and we both whirled, then relaxed. Just a bat leaving its perch outside.

I gulped, kissed Tuck more softly, and finally shot a glum look upstairs.

"All right, then." I did my best to sound confident as I turned back up the stairs. "Time to lock me up." Then I laughed. "Never thought I'd say such a thing."

Tuck grinned. "Desperate times call for desperate measures."

We kissed again on the threshold — a kiss so deep and full of longing, I nearly invited him in for the night. And I might have, if the bells hadn't rung for prayers.

Tuck groaned then drew back slowly.

"You have to go," I said, half hoping he would say no.

He nodded reluctantly. "But I'll be back. I swear I will."

I smiled. "See you soon, Friar Tuck." Then I tapped him on the lips. "Or rather, see you soon, my good knight."

Never had I seen a man look that pleased with himself. *You really think so?* his shining eyes asked.

I knew so.

"See you soon, fair maiden," he promised, then disappeared into the night.

Chapter Eight

TUCK

I didn't sleep much that night, partly from lack of time, but also due to fretting. Marian was in danger, and the clock was ticking. Her decision to remain locked up was a bold — no, a crazy one — but she was her own boss. I was just the knight — er, friar — tasked with protecting her.

Helping her, my lion growled in exasperation.

She'd insisted she could protect herself, and I respected that. But I sure wasn't going to leave anything to chance. At morning prayers, my mind spun with plans to keep as close an eye on her as possible.

So when the abbot called me in for the second time in twelve hours, I approached his office with trepidation. Was he was onto me and Marian? What if he insisted on expelling me from the abbey?

Ironic, really, that my deepest wish — leaving the clergy — had become my worst nightmare. I was the only one with the means to spring Marian from the library.

You and Father Benedict, my lion growled.

It took everything I had not to give him the evil eye as I passed him on the way into the abbot's office. I couldn't let on that I knew about Marian, and the fact that he hadn't taken the key outside the library's rear door suggested he didn't know about me.

"Good morning," I murmured to the abbot.

"Good morning," he grumbled, clearly displeased. He held up a piece of parchment. "You've been summoned to Nottingham."

I nearly choked, thinking of Lady Thornton. Was she somehow in on Prince John's plot? But if so, what did it have to do with me?

"By whom?" I sputtered.

"The sheriff." He tapped the scrolled message lying on his desk. "You're to be interviewed about that unfortunate incident two months ago."

Incident?

I scratched my chin. Which incidents did the abbot know about and which didn't he? It was hard to keep track.

"The kidnapping," he explained.

Oh, *that* incident. It was all I could do not to laugh. That was like accusing a thief of stealing a chicken, rather than the crown jewels he'd made off with a week earlier.

Robynne had helped arrange that "kidnapping" — her way of enlisting my help in sneaking a treasure trove from Nottingham to Sherwood Forest...the very treasure Marian had sent with Willa for safekeeping.

That was the amazing part — so many unconnected incidents coming together. The question was, where was it all leading?

I did my best to look grim. "Couldn't the sheriff come here?" I put a hand on my chest. "I'm still a little traumatized by it all."

His reply was a single, snippy, "No."

I had little choice but to comply, though I did help myself to Malachi, the abbey's best horse, for the trip. The sooner I was back from Nottingham, the better.

Best horse... my lion reminded me.

I detoured to Snow's stall, then called to the stableboy. "Geoffrey, move this beauty to the last stall. Abbot's orders," I bluffed.

"The one that opens to its own paddock?" he asked.

Exactly. If worse came to worst, it would be easier for Marian to make a quick getaway.

"Yes." Then I called to Rita and Rosie while saddling Malachi. "Sorry, girls. No outing today,"

"Psst."

I waved away the fly nagging at my ear.

"Psst. Tuck."

I whirled. Oh. Not a fly. Quite the opposite — it was hulking John Little, plus his mate, Willa, hidden in an empty stall.

I glanced around, checking that the stableboy was nowhere in sight, then stepped closer.

"Boy, am I glad to see you," I whispered.

"We came as fast as we could," John said.

"How is Marian?" Willa asked, clearly worried.

I glanced in the direction of the library and shook my head. "She says she's fine, but..."

When I trailed off, John sighed and glanced at his partner. "That sounds familiar."

She elbowed him. "We need to get her out. It's not safe."

"It isn't, but Marian has a different plan," I said, then explained.

John looked shocked, but Marian's crazy plan somehow made sense to Willa.

"All right. How do I get in?" she asked.

"Whoa. Wait. No," John protested.

Willa glowered. "I said, how do I get in?"

I sketched a map in the dust of the floor, indicating the safest route to the library.

"You'll have to wait until everyone is called to Sext."

John raised an eyebrow, tempting me to tell one of the many dirty jokes I'd come up with for that prayer time. But no. Gone was the joker and dreamer I'd been when I'd arrived at the abbey. Now, I felt much more like a warrior heading off on a mission. A real-life, dangerous mission, because my true love's life was on the line.

I gulped at the realization. True love? How could I be sure?

I'm sure, my lion growled. *It's destiny.*

How that worked with the *monk* thing, I had no clue. But that didn't matter right now.

"When is Sext?" John asked.

"In about two hours."

Willa's eyes went wide. "Two hours?"

The old me would have shared her impatience. But the new me was starting to understand about sacrifice.

I nodded firmly. "Two hours. Otherwise, it's too risky. Wait five minutes after the church doors shut, then head to the library. Understood?"

Willa opened her mouth, but John covered it gently with his huge hand. "Understood."

With that, I raced off on Malachi.

By mule cart, Nottingham was nearly two hours away. Malachi covered the distance in a quarter of that time. If it weren't for Marian, I would have taken a long detour just to enjoy the thrill a little longer. The sheer speed and power of a horse. The wind in my hair, the thunder of hooves over hard ground...

My heart pounded, because this wasn't a game any more. This was the real thing.

I halted a mile outside the north gate, spotting another rider charging out to meet me. Now what?

Charging turned out to be appropriate, because it was the sheriff on that dappled war-horse of his. Poor Malachi had cut a much more respectable figure beside the mules.

I sighed, and not just because of the horse. Although we were both allies of Robynne Hood, the sheriff and I didn't particularly get along, having rubbed each other the wrong way at our first meeting. We respected each other, but that was as far as the good vibes went.

"Sheriff," I growled.

"Friar." He gave me the tiniest nod.

I waited. He was the one who'd called me in, right? So why was he looking at me like that?

I jabbed my thumb over my shoulder. "If that's all you wanted, I'll be heading back now."

He frowned. "In a rush to get back to the monastery? That's a first."

If only he knew.

I stirred the air with my hand, refusing to take the bait. "You summoned me. What can I do for you?"

He cast a dark look at Nottingham's castle. "I summoned you on Lady Thornton's orders."

I froze, then covered up with a quip. "And I thought *you* were bad company."

He motioned toward the north gate. "Come. We'll talk as we ride."

We set off at a walk, quiet as we each collected our thoughts.

"Does she know about you?" I asked, keeping my voice low.

Daniel snorted. "Know about what part of me?"

Interesting. What exactly did he mean? I knew he was a dragon shifter and a secret ally of Robynne Hood. What other secrets did the man harbor?

"Shifter, I mean."

Lady Thornton, I surmised, was a wolf shifter like her brother, the late Sir Guy of Gisborne. As such, she would have identified Daniel as a dragon shifter in one quick sniff.

He circled around to ride upwind of me. "No, she doesn't know — yet."

When his scent hit me, I held a hand to my nose. "My God, man. What's that?"

He made a face. "Garlic — as much as I can stomach, plus the incense I've been burning night and day. I also stand downwind of fires and hearths every chance I get. I've told people it's my grandmother's cure for a cold coming on fast."

I chuckled. Crude, but effective. Even I couldn't pick up on the leathery scent of dragon.

My thoughts drifted to Marian. She'd hinted at being a shifter, but she didn't need to resort to such tricks to hide her scent. What species was she, then? Or maybe she wasn't a shifter at all, but a witch or a sympath. . .

I dragged my thoughts back to Daniel. "How long do you think you can keep it up?"

He scowled. "I can only hope she leaves soon."

That was the thing. Even as sheriff, Daniel had no sway over higher nobility like Lady Thornton.

I looked around, wondering what I could do to hide my scent, but Daniel shook his head.

"Not enough time, and it might play in your favor. Keep Lady Thornton guessing, if you know what I mean."

I frowned, not so sure.

"The abbot told me I'm to be interviewed about my 'kidnapping.' Why?"

Daniel's eyes flashed. "Because Lady Thornton suspects Robynne, and you're the only one known to have seen her camp."

I made a face. "And you think I'm so stupid that you need to remind me to spin a tall tale?"

He shrugged. "Maybe."

Something in me snapped, and I stopped. "Don't get all high and mighty with me, Sheriff. If I'd been free to make my own choices, I would have been off to the Crusades with the likes of you and proven myself every bit as brave."

He leveled his gaze at me, more sad than angry. "Any fool can be brave — at the beginning, when you're fresh and naive. The trick is keeping it up once you've felt — and sown — enough fear. Once you realize what the war is really about."

I frowned. "The Crusades are about seizing back the Holy Land. Everyone knows that."

Daniel laughed bitterly. "The Crusades, like most wars, are a playground for powerful men who stay far, far away from the front lines. Men who stand to profit handsomely while others suffer."

"Including King Richard?" I challenged.

Daniel nodded wearily. "I will be loyal to him to the end. But, yes. Even him, in his own way. He only risks a kingdom. But his foot soldiers — and the innocent civilians in their way — risk much, much more. Their families. Their homes. Their way of life."

I furrowed my brow. How did all that weigh up against a kingdom?

"A kingdom is abstract. Your loved ones are not," Daniel retorted. Then he growled, riding close enough to grab my robe. "You want to see action? Then look. Look hard."

I stared, wondering if he'd gone mad. But when his eyes flashed, images appeared in my mind — blurry at first, then sharper.

I saw a village consumed by an inferno. Women and children wailed, fled, or cowered helplessly at the sight of their homes going up in flames. An old man beat hopelessly at the fire. Then a mounted warrior appeared, slashing with his sword as he galloped through the village.

I winced, ready to look away.

But Daniel only tightened his grip. "Look," he ordered mercilessly.

The knight cut down the old man without so much as slowing down.

Another warrior appeared, this one on a dappled gray steed. He pulled up in front of a group of villagers who fell to their knees, begging to be spared. When he lowered his sword, my hopes rose. But then more soldiers charged up, slaughtering those poor souls before his eyes.

I saw the same warrior sliding off his horse in a different place, staring off in a daze. Wondering what he'd been part of. Asking himself why. Torturing himself with it.

"That's the action. The 'glory.' That's what the lies are made of," Daniel hissed.

More images followed. I saw a battlefield littered with bodies, not all dead. Many — most, perhaps — moaned in agony, clutching mortal wounds. When a group of men approached them, I was sure they would help. My stomach turned when they looted the battlefield instead. Some pulled boots off dying soldiers, while others laughed and tried out swords they found.

"Who helps the wounded?" I demanded, sure help would appear any moment.

"No one," Daniel said. "And any locals who survive loathe you."

"But... but..."

None of it fit what I'd dreamed about since I was a child.

"There's no honor in it," Daniel said bitterly. "No pride. No end. And no winners, except whichever cruel overlord outlives the rest."

With a little shove, he released me, and Charger broke into a trot. I stared after him, then slowly followed. Neither of us said anything for a long time.

Just before the gates, Daniel sighed and leaned closer.

"Watch what you say to Lady Thornton. She has the eyes of a hawk. The tongue of a snake. The soul of a demon."

Of that, I had no doubt.

His voice went all raspy when he added, "And whatever you do, do not reveal anything about Robynne."

His eyes flared, threatening fire and brimstone if I did.

I nodded firmly, adding *Marian* in my mind. I would conceal what I knew about her too. At the same time, I would glean what I could from Lady Thornton. What did she know? What did she have planned?

Daniel must have read my mind, because he cautioned me with a firm, "Careful. She can discover as much from the questions you pose as those you answer. Just look, listen, observe. And get the hell out of there the moment you can."

We clip-clopped over the cobblestones of the city, heading for the castle, where he left me with a final, grim look.

"Oh, and watch out. That woman could seduce the Pope — or try to, at least."

Ha. Well, not me. Not with Marian on my mind.

"Good luck," Daniel murmured.

Malachi's step faltered, telling me I would need it.

Chapter Nine

MARIAN

I didn't sleep a wink, and by morning, the nervous energy that had kept me going through the night was rapidly petering out. Still, I pushed on with improvements to the defensive systems I'd created. Even when I kept still, my mind continued pacing, going over endless possibilities.

Was I crazy for remaining here instead of grabbing my chance to escape?

But wasn't it my duty to do whatever I could to slow, if not halt, Prince John's march to power?

There's a thin line between bravery and stupidity, my father liked to say. And, boy. I was starting to see his point.

At the sound of a scratch at the back door, I leaped to my feet and grabbed my sword. The key ground in the lock as my mind slowly focused.

Back door... a silent visitor... Tuck?

"Wait!" I cried as the door creaked open.

"Marian?"

I froze. Wait. Not Tuck. A woman. Someone I knew...

"Willa!" I called. "Whoa — wait!"

I lunged forward to halt the bookshelf I'd rigged to topple if anyone arrived unannounced. It had been simple enough to lever it up on one side with a piece of firewood, wedge at a precarious angle with books, and finally connect to the door with braided fibers from my needlepoint project. But it was twice as tall as me and filled with hundreds of heavy volumes, so stopping it once the trap had been sprung was another matter.

"Help!" I squeaked.

Lord, the irony. I would be killed by my own booby trap rather than meeting a noble death in service of my country.

Willa darted to my side, and we both groaned under the weight. Even if that bookshelf didn't crush us when it fell, the noise would bring Father Benedict running.

"Mind if I help?" a deep voice asked cautiously.

Was he kidding?

Please do, I nearly yelled.

But Willa only croaked out a reluctant, "If you must."

That was Willa, all right.

The weight instantly eased from my straining arms and the bookshelf creaked back upright. A huge man dusted his hands and pinned Willa with a stern look.

"We had it under control," she grumbled.

"Clearly," he murmured.

Despite the words, their banter had a loving tone. Still, I kept a hand on my dagger. "Who are you?"

He pointed to Willa. "I'm with her."

Willa touched my arm. "He is. That's John. My...um...er..."

Friend? Lover? Mate? The way their eyes glowed when they looked at each other told me all three applied.

I stared for a moment. Well, well. *I don't want and will never need a man* Willa had found someone who changed her mind.

Then my eyes went wide, because my nose had just processed something in her scent.

Shifter. *Bear* shifter was my best bet. Both of them.

I shouldn't have been surprised that Willa hadn't just found just any man, but a big, hulking bear shifter with the arms of a lumberjack and legs like tree trunks.

"Oh." I stepped back. "Hello."

He raised an eyebrow in the direction of the bookshelf.

"Just in case," I explained, pointing to the other door. "Don't go near there either. Oh, and don't touch that chair...or that candelabra...or that rug."

His jaw fell open, and I nearly rolled my eyes. Yes, I'd booby-trapped them all. Did he think I would sit around twiddling my thumbs while waiting to be rescued?

"Tuck sent us. We came as quickly as we could. Oh, Marian!" Willa threw her arms around me.

I hugged her back, and we hung on, rocking from side to side.

"So good to see you're all right," I said, fighting away tears of relief.

Willa was my best friend, my sparring partner, and my co-conspirator in countless childhood escapades. More recently, I'd had no choice but to send Willa on a dangerous mission to deliver my family's greatest treasures for safekeeping with Robin Hood.

"You made it. You did it," I congratulated her.

Willa grinned, touching her partner's arm. "I had some help." Then her expression fell. "Oh — what about Beverly? Did she make it home safely?"

I grinned at that reminder of my sweetest, dimmest lady-in-waiting. "Yes. She's probably designing outfits and hairstyles for me as we speak."

We both laughed.

"So, you've met the elusive Robin Hood," I said, a little jealous. "What's he like?"

Willa grinned. "Not he. She."

My eyes went wide. "Boy, do we have a lot to catch up on."

Willa laughed, winding her arm around John's. "We do."

He eyed the door warily. "Soon. But first, we need to get you out of here."

I shook my head. "I can't leave."

It took some time to explain, but they finally understood my master plan. Well, Willa did. She even insisted on staying with me as backup. My instinct was to protest, because why endanger her too? But, lord. Even I knew when I needed a friend at my side.

"Too dangerous," John protested. "For both of you."

"Maybe, but the plan makes sense," Willa said. "The longer we buy Marian's allies time, the better chance they have of defeating Prince John. And anyway, what's really dangerous is for her to remain alone." She bumped shoulders with me and grinned. "Together, the two of us make a pretty imposing force. And not just when it comes to setting booby traps."

"I have no doubt," he said. "But it's still too much to risk."

Willa pulled something out of her pocket and pressed it into my hand. "There's this, too."

I gasped, holding it up. "The Ring of Aquitaine!"

"It works. It really works," Willa whispered. "When I needed it most, it helped."

The moment I slid it onto my finger, I felt its warmth and hidden power. Which was comforting, but frightening too. How soon might I have to call upon it?

It took a lot of convincing, but we eventually talked John into keeping guard over the back stairs while Willa and I hunkered down in the library, trying to plan for every eventuality. When Tuck returned — soon, I hoped — we would all meet to take stock.

"I just hope he's not kept long in Nottingham," I fretted.

"If it's the sheriff who called him in, it's fine. He's on our side," Willa assured me.

Wow. Robynne Hood had built a truly formidable network. Still, with Lady Thornton in Nottingham...

"That woman is bad news," John grumbled.

"That woman is also a wolf shifter," I warned. "Not to be underestimated in any way."

Willa went still. "You know about shifters?"

I shooed John toward the back door, then winked at my friend. "Like I said, we have a lot to catch up on. Shall I go first, or do you want to?"

Willa's eyes were wide. "You first. Because this, I have to hear."

Chapter Ten

TUCK

Outside the castle, it was cold and gloomy. Inside wasn't much better. And when I was ushered into the great hall, the air all but crackled with malice.

"Lady Thornton," I murmured, dropping into a deep bow.

She snapped her fingers, prompting the staff to scurry away. Massive oak doors slammed shut behind me, and the sound echoed through the hall.

"Friar Tuck."

Her tone was flat, and I could feel her eyes prodding me like a new specimen on a dissection dish.

Silence stretched, playing games with my mind. What had I already given away? My practiced bow would have told her about the high standing of the family I'd been born into, while my robe spoke of where I was now and why. And my scent...

"Well, well..." she murmured, circling me like a hawk — or a wolf, I supposed. "Lion shifter. How very noble."

I kept my eyes on the floor, waiting as her glittery shoes made one pass after another.

Then, out of nowhere, she laughed. "You're wasted in the clergy."

No kidding, I could have sighed. Though, after the images Daniel had shared with me, I was rethinking the *brave knight* thing. Maybe I could find something more worthy. Something closer to home. Something I could be in control of rather than being a puppet in the all-too-real theater of a powerful man's games...

Lady Thornton snapped her fingers at me. "Look at me."

A woman accustomed to barking orders. Well, I could pretend I loved to obey — especially since the abbot wasn't there to set the record straight.

I kept my eyes straight ahead as she circled in and out of my view. For a few seconds, I saw long, flowing black hair and a pinched, haughty face. Then when she continued her endless circles — like a mule hitched to a mill, though I didn't say as much — my eyes focused on the animal heads mounted on the wall beyond. Ghostly eyes saw through me, antlers jabbed in my direction, and teeth showed in eternal snarls. Snarls that accused me of doing that to them.

I wished I could proclaim my innocence. Then I thought of the villagers Daniel encountered during the Crusades. Had he felt the same when forced to confront them?

"I've been wondering..." Lady Thornton spoke slowly, giving me too much time to wonder what she'd wondered, over and over in an endless loop with no beginning and no end.

I counted the sets of antlers on the wall. Seven...eight...nine...

"Wondering about a lion shifter, young and well-built..." she practically purred those last few words.

I gritted my teeth. Was this how Marian felt when people commented on her beauty, her figure, her grace? And, ugh. I pictured being an attractive young woman circled by a much older, much more powerful man, uttering the same suggestive message in the same seductive tone.

Ugh. My lion grimaced the way he did when he coughed up hair balls.

My brothers had once joked that women had it easy. Now, I wasn't so sure.

"And yet, you were overcome and kidnapped by the outlaws of Sherwood Forest," Lady Thornton finished.

Oops. I hadn't considered how that would look.

"Well?" she demanded.

I looked at her directly for the first time. "Is that a statement or a question?"

And, oops. Hadn't Daniel warned me not to give anything away? Being defensive suggested I had something to hide.

"In the abbey, we're expected to remain silent unless asked a direct question," I added, covering up quickly.

"Ah. So obedient." Her voice was dry. "Then I shall ask, as you request. How is it that a lion as capable as you could be so easily overcome by a few outlaws?"

"They promised not to hurt anyone if I cooperated, and I didn't want to endanger an innocent person."

"So noble," she dripped. Then she tapped her lips, speaking more to herself than to me. "Not a bad strategy."

I stared. She didn't mean *my* strategy. She meant the idea of blackmail. God, how sick was she?

More silence ensued. More circling. I forced myself not to shift from foot to foot.

"Tell me about Robin Hood and his camp," she finally ordered.

Her camp, I wished I could say. Then I regurgitated the details I'd invented months ago for Daniel's official report. I'd been blindfolded, I claimed, with no sense of where the camp lay. And the scene I described after the blindfold was removed had no relation to the truth. Neither did the number of outlaws, which I multiplied by ten.

It was terrifying, I nearly embellished but decided not to. Better to stick close to the truth.

Which meant picturing John Little when I described Robin Hood. Not anywhere as brilliant as the real Robynne, but hey. He fit the image most people painted in their minds.

"I see," Lady Thornton said in that lazy hiss of hers. "In other words, you're as much help to me as the sheriff."

Not helpful at all, her tone complained.

Then she switched back to a seductive purr. "Have a think. Is there anything you might have left out?"

I made a show of thinking it over, then shrugged. "That's all."

"And what about Maid Marian?"

The question came out of nowhere, and I nearly jolted. A good thing Lady Thornton had paced behind me at that moment.

"What about her, m'lady?"

"I understand she's a guest of the abbey."

My lion growled inside. *If this bitch has a spy in the abbey, I'll kill him.*

I played dumb, of course. "Is she? That would explain that fancy horse in the stable."

"Is that where you work?"

I shook my head. "I work in the brewery and in the garden."

And never, ever the library, my lion wanted to add, as if that would help.

A good thing my human side was being interrogated and not him.

"Ah, a man who works with his hands," she hummed, running a hand over my back. Lower, lower...

I did my best not to flinch, or sigh in relief when her hand slipped away again. But that brought her face-to-face with me, and she stopped, much too close.

I stood perfectly still while Lady Thornton waited for her beauty and power to do their work. A realistic enough expectation, because she was beautiful — except for that pinched expression of hers — and potent, like poisonous mushrooms that lured you in by mimicking the edible kind.

Her dubious charms pinged off my imaginary armor like dull arrows, falling harmlessly to the ground. I focused on the mounted badger head behind her, taking its cue not to blink.

With a frown and an audible *hmpf,* Lady Thornton resumed her ominous walk.

"Back to Maid Marian..." she started.

"The most beautiful woman in the land," I supplied. "Or so I hear."

Her shoe scraped over the stone floor. "So I keep hearing, too," she said bitterly.

Well, maybe don't scowl as much, I wanted to say. *And try to be nice.*

"But is she cunning? Ambitious? Powerful?" Lady Thornton demanded.

Yes, yes, and yes, I decided, though the questions were rhetorical. Also, Marian's ambitions were in a whole different category to this snake's.

But I kept my answer to a neutral, "I suppose you're a better judge than I."

"Of course I am. But I am also in need of a second pair of eyes, and yours would be perfect."

I went stiff. Perfect for what?

"Tell me everything you have seen or heard since her arrival in the abbey," she demanded.

"Unfortunately, I haven't seen anything — except the horse, if it is hers — and the only word I've heard of her visit is what you've just said. I'm sorry."

"Think carefully, my dear lion," Lady Thornton all but hissed in my ear. "Think about how useful you could be to me, and I to you."

That caught my attention. "Useful?"

Lady Thornton smiled that viper smile.

"Indeed. You report her movements, habits, and visitors to me. In return, I will reward you handsomely."

"Reward me? How?"

I had no intention of taking her up on the offer, but I was curious about what she thought I could be bribed with.

She leaned in, whispering in the playful tone of a lover. "In any manner you wish. Riches. Privilege. Even freedom from that place."

My heart skipped a beat.

"Come now. We both know you are destined for greater things than a monk's life," she went on, practically fondling my ear.

"But my vows..." I asked, testing her.

She snorted. "I can secure you a royal dispensation. Say, an immediate transfer to a decorated unit on the front lines of the Crusades?"

The irony killed me. For months, I'd desperately wanted to quit the clergy. Now, I had two offers to do so — and I couldn't accept either!

Plus, *royal dispensation* suggested Lady Thornton considered herself in with Prince John — the very man conspiring to steal the throne. Was she in cahoots with the prince's scheme to grab power?

"So, what do you say?" she asked.

A tiny piece of my heart died as I uttered my only option. "Thank you, but my place is in the abbey."

Words I never thought I'd hear myself say, but there they were. I had to remain at the abbey — at least, as long as Marian was there.

Lady Thornton scoffed, sending a puff of air into my ear. I winced.

"Poverty, obedience, chastity." She emphasized the latter with a pat to my ass. "You'd rather suffer through a lifetime of that than accept your just reward?"

Actually, I was desperate for my just reward. But Lady Thornton wasn't the one to determine what that might be.

I shrugged. "I'm sorry, m'lady. I fear I am of little use to you."

The door opened just then, and a footman entered with a message. I used the opportunity to stride for the door.

The words she called after me chilled me to the bone.

"Little use? Don't be too sure, my dear lion."

Chapter Eleven

MARIAN

I was on pins and needles the rest of the day. For all that I loved having Willa with me — and her hulking partner just outside the door — it was hard not to worry. Prince John...what was he up to? My allies, such as Lord Winthrop, whom I was counting on to rally more supporters...were they finally on the move? Then there was that bitch Lady Thornton...what was her role in all this?

Most of all, Tuck...was he all right? What was happening in Nottingham?

I touched the Ring of Aquitaine, hoping for some comfort.

Then I imagined Tuck was with me, nice and close. Not just for comfort, but more. More...

My body heated, and my cheeks burned. Well, maybe not with Willa and John around. I was glad to have them with me now, but when Tuck returned...maybe I could send them down to the scriptorium to peruse some parchments or something. Willa could read, and if John couldn't, he could listen to her read aloud. Surely they'd find that engrossing for an hour or two...maybe even all night.

Because I wanted that time with Tuck. No, I *burned* for it.

But, damn. He wasn't with me at the moment, and even if he were, he was a monk.

I sighed. Destiny must hate me.

My animal side, though, held out hope. *Destiny will smile upon us. You'll see.*

I pursed my lips, finding that hard to believe.

When a knock sounded at the back door, I jumped to my feet. Willa grabbed a dagger, then sniffed the air and relaxed.

"It's John. . .and Tuck."

Funny, I'd just come to the same conclusion. A sixth sense had told me.

My breath caught. Willa knew because John was her mate. I knew because. . .Tuck was mine?

Destiny, a faint voice whispered in my mind.

It had to be, because when he entered, it was like the sun breaking out of the clouds after a week of gloom.

"Don't touch that," John Little warned Tuck. "Not the door. Not the bookshelf either. Oh, and don't get close to that rug." Then he sighed. "Just don't touch anything." Finally, he dropped his voice. "And watch what you say. These are two women you don't want to tick off."

Tuck gave him a look that asked if John had spent a little too much time in the woods, then waved at Willa and turned to me.

He beamed — at me, for me, with me — and stepped close.

After exactly two seconds of trying to restrain myself, I threw myself into a hug. Tuck laughed and hugged me back, long, close, and warm.

I was aware of Willa and John going a little wide-eyed. And heck, I was a little surprised too. But there was no denying the attraction I felt for the man, and no rules for how fast — or slow — love ought to work. Plus, Willa and John went all dreamy-eyed around each other. Couldn't Tuck and I do the same?

For a moment, my soul soared. Then it crashed again. Willa could have John because he wasn't a monk. Tuck was.

I released him and smoothed my hands over my dress.

"Good to see you back safely."

His smile was just as sad and wistful. "Good to see you safe too."

"What did the sheriff want?" Willa asked.

"I wasn't interrogated by the sheriff. It was Lady Thornton. And, Lord. I thought Sir Guy was bad. . ."

"What is she plotting now?" John asked.

Tuck made to flop into a chair, but John grabbed him first and looked at me.

"That one is safe," I assured him.

John released Tuck, who slumped down wearily. "What is she plotting? Hard to tell, but she wanted to know about your camp." Willa and John looked at each other while Tuck turned to me. "And she wanted to know about you."

I tried playing it cool despite the ice that sent down my spine. "Did she now?"

Tuck nodded. "She knows you're here."

I made a face. "News travels fast."

"Father Benedict," Tuck cursed, then went on. "She wanted me to spy on you."

I snorted. "I'm locked in a library. What is there to spy on — which books I read?"

Tuck shrugged. "I played dumb, telling her I haven't seen or heard anything."

He and I exchanged a secret glance. Not only had he seen and heard, he'd touched and kissed. Two things I was dying for more of.

Tuck smacked his thighs, signaling a call to action. "Well, it's clear we have to get you out of here."

That was where things got a little sticky. As before, Willa was on board with my plan, while John was not.

"It's too dangerous," both men said at the same time.

I glowered at them. "So, it's all right for men to rush off to the Crusades or other heroic deeds. But when a woman wants to do anything more dangerous than needlepoint, it's out of the question."

John eyed the needle I'd left out for easy access and muttered, "I bet you could make needlepoint dangerous."

Willa elbowed him in the ribs.

"Oof," he groaned. "What? It's true."

I stuck my hands on my hips. "That's exactly my point. I am *capable*. More than most soldiers. And duty calls as strongly to me as it does to any man."

Tuck patted the air with his hands. "I agree. I'm just saying, making yourself a sitting duck isn't the best way of going about that."

"Then what would you have me do?"

"Leave while you can. Ride out and rally your allies. Make sure they're setting things in motion instead of assuming they will."

"I would like nothing better. But if I escape, the news will travel fast, and Prince John will hunt me down and stamp out any hint of resistance. Any ally I contact will become a target, and if they are cut down, the others will give in. They're loyal to King Richard, but they won't be willing to sacrifice everything without a strong chance of success."

"And yet you are," Tuck noted.

The room went quiet.

I nodded slowly. "Yes, I am. I must. It's my duty."

Silence reigned for the next few minutes as everyone swallowed that — including me. Because, yikes. It was one thing to *plan* to act nobly. It was another to actually do so.

Then Willa broke the silence with a faint murmur. "As long as Prince John thinks you're safely locked up here..."

I cocked my head, as did the men.

A mischievous expression came over her face, and John groaned.

"Oh no, you don't."

Tuck and I looked on quizzically while they argued.

"It's a great idea!" Willa insisted.

"It's a terrible idea," John growled.

"What idea?" Tuck whispered.

I shrugged. "No clue."

"I can do it," Willa went on.

"You can, but you won't," John said. "Come on, Willa. This is like you rushing to Nottingham to get the treasure yourself."

Tuck looked at me, but I had no idea what *that* was about.

"It's totally different," Willa insisted. "Because I'll have help. You."

"Not enough," John stressed.

Tuck shushed them, pointing to the front door. "Quiet, now. Lady Thornton didn't enlist me to spy, but she might have found someone else."

Willa motioned for everyone to huddle, then whispered, "I could stay and pretend to be Marian, while she heads out and rallies the resistance."

"You don't look anything like her," Tuck said. "And you're much smaller."

John and I both backed out of striking range, knowing how Willa was likely to react.

"I'm not small!"

Tuck fluttered his hands. "Of course not. It's just that she's big."

"Big?" I bristled. "In what way?"

Tuck looked at John for help, but the bear shifter gave him a look that said, *You're on your own against these two.*

"I meant... Forget it. What I'm trying to say is, they won't buy it."

I wasn't totally sold on the idea either, but it did have some merit. "Father Benedict is the only one who's ever entered — besides Tuck."

Tuck made a face. "You never know. Cyril might come wandering in here looking for more art." At Willa's quizzical look, he explained, "Another monk. Great singer, dirty-minded artist. He keeps hoping to start a choir here. We prefer art lessons... not that the abbot has approved either."

Willa shrugged. "It doesn't matter who enters. I could stay on the couch under a blanket, hiding behind Marian's needlepoint." Her eyes flashed. "And if someone discovers our switch, I'll skewer them with the needle."

"I'll kill them first," John growled.

And just like that, we had the makings of a plan. One even crazier than before, but heck. It could work. There was just one thing...

"I hate putting you in danger again." I touched Willa's arm. "After delivering the treasure, I mean."

She grinned at me, then John. "Well, that worked out well, don't you think?"

Funny how a big, fierce man could go all dopey at just a few words.

"It did," he whispered. "It certainly did."

Willa gazed at her mate a moment longer. "The best things in life happen when you least expect them."

"True," Tuck granted. "But I'm not sure that's the best motto to head into battle with. Because that's what this will be. Us against Prince John — and probably Lady Thornton. The only question is, are the two of them working together or against each other?"

I made a face. "Knowing her, she'll join forces while it's convenient, then strike when the prince's back is turned."

Everyone froze — even me.

"Wait. Could that really be her plan?" I whispered.

Tuck jutted his jaw. "It makes sense — from her point of view. She's jealous of you..."

I made a face. She could join a whole club of jealous women. If only they walked a day in my shoes...

"And she's power hungry," he finished.

John nodded thoughtfully. "They say she killed off two husbands already. Maybe she's angling for a third."

Willa frowned. "What do you mean?"

Tuck took over from there, mulling over the possibilities.

"Prince John wants to force Marian to marry him. That would eliminate her as an enemy and gain him the prestige of her family name."

I scowled, though I didn't disagree.

"Let's say Lady Thornton helps him with that," Tuck continued. "He appreciates her help..."

"She kills me off..." I added dryly.

"...and then makes her move on Prince John," Willa said, looking startled. "Husband number three. Then, once he's successfully eliminated all opposition, she bumps him off, and she's left in charge."

Everyone went still.

"Honestly. Is she that ruthless? That thirsty for power?" I asked.

John and Tuck answered at the same time. "Absolutely."

Chapter Twelve

TUCK

"This way," I whispered, leading Marian outside. Cold night air bit my cheeks, and every shadow seemed to harbor a lurking enemy. My only comfort was the warmth of Marian's hand in mine.

Mine. My lion echoed that word.

I reminded myself that even if I wasn't a monk, Marian was way, way out of my league. Because there was noble, and there was *noble.* I was only the third son of my minorly aristocratic family — no matter how much my father liked to hint at a personal friendship with the king. Marian, meanwhile, was the one and only child of Lord William of Newton, and the king's goddaughter, to boot.

Still, something inside me clung to hope. The self-defeating part, I feared.

Focus, my lion growled.

Right. I looked around, then hurried onward. I couldn't count how many times I'd snuck around the abbey grounds at night, but this was different. This was definitely not a game, nor a fantasy. This was the real thing. Marian's life was in danger — and now, the lives of Willa and John too. Every action I took had a direct impact on the success — or failure — of our crazy plan.

"Faster," Marian urged.

I shook my head. Every second was precious, but one misstep now could sink our ship before it left the dock.

I peered around, then rushed across the lawn to the next point of cover — a dark wall by the refectory. I winced at the crunch of our feet over frosty ground, then pressed myself against the stonework. Heart pounding, I peered back the way we'd come. No sound, no movement. Just us.

When Marian looked back and upward, her throat bobbed. A moment later, I did the same. That was the library over there, sheltering our friends. Friends who'd put themselves in mortal danger for a higher cause.

I pictured Father Benedict entering with breakfast in the morning. Surely he wouldn't be fooled by the switch, even if Willa kept herself hidden. Or, what if he tightened security and sent someone up the back stairs? John would be discovered, and the alarm would be raised. Or what if—

Marian squeezed my hand. "Have faith. They can handle anything that comes up."

My faith in them was unshakable — but not my faith in fate.

Still, Marian was right. We were all soldiers in the same army, and we had to trust one another to manage our respective roles. Which meant getting a move on, at least for me and Marian.

We rushed across the next open space, then tiptoed around the forge to reach the back gate. There, we glanced back one more time.

When a horse nickered in the stable, Marian whispered sadly. "Snow..."

We'd considered, then discarded the idea of taking horses. If they were discovered missing, everyone's suspicions would be aroused.

When Snow grew restless, Marian closed her eyes and lifted her hand, as if the horse were right there.

"Shh..." she whispered into the night air. "Everything will be all right."

There was no way Snow could see or hear her from inside the stable. But the mare immediately settled down. It was uncanny.

Marian gulped and wiped away a tear. "Let's go."

After a last peek around, we stole outside the abbey walls and started down the dark road. At first, we race-walked, keeping our steps quiet. Then we jogged and finally broke into a run. After half a mile, I stopped, shaking my head at miles of open territory ahead.

"Are you sure Winthrop is the best option?" I asked.

"It's our only option," Marian insisted.

We'd gone over it all in the library. Lord Winthrop was her father's oldest friend and a staunch supporter of the king. He was also the only person with enough standing — and enough loyal footmen — to get word to everyone else quickly and quietly.

Still, Winthrop was miles away.

"We'll never make it before dawn. Not at this rate. Maybe we could steal some horses..."

Marian shook her head. We'd been over that too. Even in an emergency, she wasn't willing to steal from honest folk. My own fault for introducing her to the locals, I suppose.

"Are you telling me a lion can't run through the night?" she huffed.

Now that put my tail in a twist. "Of course I can. But what about you?"

"Oh, I can definitely run as fast as a horse, and all through the night."

I tilted my head. How exactly did she plan to pull that off?

"Oh, ye of no faith." She tossed her head and threw back the monk's robe I'd given her as a disguise.

I stared. "What are you doing?"

She gave me a firm look. "Trusting you. With my life. With the future of the kingdom. And now, with my family's greatest secret."

The air shimmered around her shoulders as she shed layers of clothing. My breath caught. Up until then, my best guess as to her true nature had tended toward *witch* or *sympath*. But that shimmer was the sure sign of a shift.

I held my breath, watching, waiting. What kind of shifter had no telltale scent? What species could run through the night as far and as fast as a horse?

"Hm-hmm." She cleared her throat.

I blushed and turned at that silent command. She was down to her undergarments by then, and those would be next.

A moment later, a bundle landed by my feet. "Would you be able to carry those?" she asked. "I'll need them later."

I nodded dumbly, knowing I ought to shift too. But at that moment, I was too frozen in anticipation to move.

Most shifters produced a little groan while transforming, because bone and muscle didn't rearrange without making themselves felt. But Marian didn't make a sound. When her feet scuffed over the frozen ground, I strained to identify what I heard. Four clunky feet, by the sound of it, because the scuffing was louder than the sound made by paws. Then came a little murmur, and I turned slowly.

Come along, already, Marian chided, using mind-talk that was faint at first, then clearer. *Shift. There's no time to waste.*

There wasn't, but holy hell. All I could do was stare.

Four dainty hooves. A long, silky mane as dark as her human hair. Wide nostrils, intelligent eyes the same color as a starry night.

I stared and stared and stared.

Horse shifters were rare, but Marian was something rarer still.

"Unicorn," I breathed, watching as the spiral of her single, long horn reached its full length. The white of it contrasted with the black of her body and the inky night.

"You're a unicorn," I sputtered.

Marian tossed her head in an exact duplicate of the motion she made in human form.

What keen eyes you have. Can we go now?

I didn't move. I couldn't.

Only the oldest, most noble family lines carried unicorn blood, and that only came out once every few generations. Black unicorns were rarer still, or so I'd heard. And frankly, I'd put the whole lot down to folklore.

But there she stood in the flesh. The wind made her silky tail sway, and her coat, like her eyes, shone under the starlight. Near the tip of her horn, a single band of gold glinted.

The Ring of Aquitaine, a distant corner of my mind said.

It took her muttering "Men!" and cantering off for me to finally break into action.

I wrapped our clothes into a bundle that I strapped loosely to my back, then shifted. That little trick had taken me ages to master — arranging the straps in the right positions for my lion body. Then I shook out my mane and sprinted after her.

I was panting by the time I caught up, because boy, could that unicorn run. Although I did suspect a little showboating, because Marian gradually settled into a more sustainable pace. Even then... Wow. I'd never seen a horse with a smoother gait.

Of course, I'd never seen a horse with a horn either.

When I tripped for the fourth time — a consequence of secretly watching her from the corner of my eye — Marian tossed that silky mane.

Everything all right?

I gave a jerky nod and stared straight ahead.

Sheep turned to watch us pass, and birds circled overhead. I couldn't blame them. It wasn't often one saw a unicorn prance by with a lion at her side.

Marian towered above me, gliding along gracefully, while I ran at her side in a long, feline lope. We detoured around farms and villages where horses nickered in wonder and glee. At one point, we passed three huge draft horses in a field, and the trio lined up, bowing their heads.

I gaped, because that sure as hell wasn't out of deference to me.

Let me guess. You're their queen, I ventured.

She sighed. *Something like that.*

I frowned. *Why do you sound frustrated? Isn't that nice?*

She snorted — a doubly powerful one, now that she was in equine form. *All my life, I've been praised for things I can't control — beauty, wealth, noble standing. Just once, I'd like to be judged by things I've worked hard for. Like knowledge. Diplomacy. Charitable work...*

Swordsmanship, I filled in. *Setting booby traps. You're a master when it comes to those.*

The rhythm of her hoofbeats hitched for a moment, and her eyes glowed in pride.

I do my best, she murmured modestly.

We ran in silence for a while, but eventually, I chuckled.

What? she demanded.

I eyed her horn. *Must be handy to have a weapon with you at all times.*

She huffed. *You try fighting with a sword attached to your head.*

With that, she tossed her head left and right, mimicking a sword. And while her movements were as graceful as everything else she did, I could see her point. That horn might be lethal, but it was a little too long and high to be of practical use.

True, I finally said. *And poor you. Your tail isn't even tufted.* I gave mine a proud snap. *I don't know how you survive.*

She laughed. *Yes, poor me.*

I knew what she meant, though. I didn't like being judged by my family, my looks, or my wealth either. Then I chuckled. That was one good thing about the clergy — no one cared about all that. Plus, the people I met — locals like Bess or Robynne and the Merry Men — only cared about my deeds.

So, there. I'd finally found one upside to joining the clergy.

Then my heart sank. One measly upside stacked against dozens of minuses that would deny me my mate forever.

After that, it was Marian eyeing me as I ran in silence, staring sullenly ahead.

We ran all night, fueled by the urgency of our mission. After a while, the landscape blurred, though that could have been from the handful of rogue tears I shed. I barely even noticed dawn breaking over the horizon or how the settlements we passed steadily grew more dense. It was only when we crested a rise that we stopped and gazed ahead.

"Winthrop," Marian breathed.

I studied the hilltop town a few miles away. A ring of stout walls guarded the base, and a jagged line of roofs climbed the natural slope. At the summit stood a castle — the kind built for war, not show, though the flags flapping above each tower softened the impression a bit.

I squinted, studying the flags. Most showed a red field guarded by three golden lions — the royal standard used by both King Richard and Prince John. But the tallest tower flew a second flag beneath that one. The red-and-white cross of Saint George — the flag King Richard fought under in the Crusades.

Those flags had been flown everywhere when the king had first departed for the Holy Land. But the more power Prince John snatched, the rarer that sight had become, more out of fear than lack of support. But Lord Winthrop didn't appear to have any qualms about making his position clear. He might as well have positioned a dozen trumpeters on the castle walls to blast "God Save the King" — with an extra stanza that said, *Yes, the king, not his usurping brother.*

Almost there, Marian murmured.

Her voice was wary, as was I. Traitors lurked everywhere — maybe even here.

Never had I had such a sense of fate looming over me. Never had I wondered so intensely if I would live to see the next day.

Our eyes locked, and there was so much I yearned to say, from *I love you* to *You don't have to do this* and even a slightly lame, *Wow, you're a unicorn,* because I still wasn't completely over the shock.

But all I managed was a throaty growl. *This may be friendly territory, but I still don't like the feel of this.*

Marian pranced in place. *What's to like?*

Still, we started down the hill a moment later, headed for that castle — and our destiny, whatever that would prove to be.

Chapter Thirteen

MARIAN

"Tea, sir? Miss?"

I glanced up from the map I'd been poring over with Lord and Lady Winthrop.

I blinked at Jacobs, their butler. Hadn't we just had tea?

A glance out the window revealed a rapidly dimming landscape. Was it already sunset?

I'd spent the day strategizing, sending messages, and plotting with the Winthrops. Well, maybe not *plotting*, because that was aimed at deposing a king. I aimed to keep Richard on the throne — and I wouldn't mind saving my own skin either. Because if Prince John succeeded in snatching the throne, he would also snatch *me*.

The thought of a forced marriage to that horrible man made me sick. I could hold my own in a fair fight, but Prince John was notorious for *dirty*. I would have no chance, and it was all too easy to imagine the horrors I would be subjected to.

The worst was knowing that to die fighting him — a fate I preferred to a life under that brute of a man — wouldn't do anything to improve life for others. Townsfolk everywhere would be subject to the same cruel practices.

Somehow, I had to succeed in my plan.

We must succeed, my unicorn side agreed.

I glanced over to the tiny chapel that opened to the great hall via a sliding wooden door. Tuck was there, doing more pacing than praying, and wow. Even in his friar's robe, he looked more knightly than ever.

I shot him a tight smile, and his eyes glowed.

My heart thumped, and a voice in the back of my mind whispered, *My destined mate.*

My unicorn pranced with the thought, but the rest of me mourned. Destiny must have a twisted sense of humor, because Tuck was a priest *and* we were likely to die soon anyway.

Tuck kept his mournful eyes on mine for another few heartbeats. Then he shook his head and whispered into my mind.

No, we won't. We'll find a way through this — somehow.

Another messenger entered and bowed to Lord Winthrop — one of many who had come and gone all day. Winthrop took the note, then dismissed the man with a nod. He read the message quickly, then showed it to me.

"Lord Ainsworth is with us. He can assemble his men in three days."

Three days? I wanted to wail. Three days could be too late.

"No word yet from Woodborough, but Lindby is with us too," he added.

I glanced at Tuck, who kept his lips pursed, his gaze distant.

Winthrop sipped his tea. "We must be patient."

I gritted my teeth. Lord Winthrop was a good man, but like so many old-timers, he moved at a glacial pace. Didn't he know the clock was ticking?

But his gaze was distant, his brow furrowed. He was probably well aware of that, but accepted there was nothing more we could do to hurry things up.

The next two hours ticked by in the same vein. Wax dripped from candles like so many slow waterfalls in a sleepy, alternative world. My shoulders ached, and my eyes went drier and drier. It had been a long day.

At some point, Winthrop sighed and stood. "You do your father proud, my dear."

The words warmed me, because I'd spent the first two hours of the day getting him to take me seriously. By afternoon, he'd been calling me by my father's name, then hastily correcting himself. *William — er, Marian, I mean...*

"I agree," Lady Winthrop said. "But even your father would agree there is little more we can accomplish today." With that, she blew out one candle, then another.

I cupped the next few with my hands before she extinguished those too, along with my drooping hopes. But she was right, and I knew it.

I sighed and blew them out myself.

"Good night. And thank you," I added quickly, reminding myself the Winthrops had as much to lose as anyone — starting with their heads. "For everything."

Lord Winthrop's smile was genuine. "No, thank *you*." Then he looked over at Tuck and raised his voice. "And thank you, Friar. Jacobs can show you to the chapel for evening prayers."

Tuck stuck up his hands as fast as a knight blocking an incoming blow. "Not necessary." Then he caught himself. "I mean, I'll find it myself."

"As you wish," Winthrop murmured, leaving the room with a half-hidden grin. "Good night."

God, I hoped he wasn't onto us. Him or sweet Lady Winthrop, who showed me to a room for the night.

"You should be comfortable enough here. And you, Friar..."

I steeled myself for her to lead him to a different part of the castle.

"As you're a man of God, I'm sure you'd rather lodge with the priest in the local church, so as not to miss prayers," Lady Winthrop started.

Tuck's stricken face implied he'd get a better night's sleep in a cow shed, but she went on before he could force a polite reply.

"But I must insist you take that room." Lady Winthrop motioned to a door across the hall. "It will make me feel better to have a man as powerful — er, pious — as you near our dear Marian, should any need arise."

I stared. Tuck stared. Lady Winthrop winked and pressed a candlestick into my hand. "Anything else you might need before going to bed?"

"No," we practically shouted in unison.

Lady Winthrop chuckled and turned away. "Good. Then I bid you both a restful night."

My cheeks heated. Tuck shifted his weight from foot to foot. We listened as her footsteps receded around the corner and up the stairs. Then everything went quiet, and the only motion was the shadows my candle cast over the walls.

I gulped and looked at Tuck.

Just the two of you now, the flickering light seemed to say. *All alone.*

His throat bobbed, and his hands formed fists.

"Long day," he finally murmured.

I nodded. Long and slow enough to give my libido time to imagine better pastimes. Throughout lunch, I'd pictured stealing away to a quiet corner for a quick tryst with Tuck. Given how slowly Lord Winthrop ate, we would have had plenty of time.

And while I'd dutifully concentrated on plans, allies, and enemies throughout the afternoon, I'd stolen a few moments to imagine myself and Tuck lying naked on the rug before that huge fireplace. On the desk, too. Up against the wall...

Don't worry, my dear, Lord Winthrop had murmured at about that time. *Everything will be all right.*

I'd nodded quickly. If only he knew where my dirty mind had been.

But that was nothing compared to where my mind flew now that Tuck and I were alone.

"I should go. Good night." His voice was tight.

I didn't move or speak. Instead, I willed him to slide closer and kiss me.

The glow in his eyes intensified, and I pictured a devil on one shoulder and an angel on the other, both fighting for his soul.

For the first time in my life, I sided with the devil. What did angels know about sweet, sinful surrender? What did they know about passion and need?

But maybe Tuck's angel was an exception, because his body practically trembled with the effort of restraint, as if both those voices were pushing him toward me.

Finally, he jerked away and walked stiffly toward the other room.

"Tuck," I whispered.

His steps remained resolute, all the way to the other door, which he opened with a creak. Then he disappeared, and it closed with a thump. I pictured him leaning against the inside, panting.

Then I pictured him inside me, panting in a whole different way.

And, *bang!* The door flew open so hard, it hit the wall, and Tuck rushed back to me.

My chuckle turned into a moan as his mouth covered mine. Seconds later, he had me pressed hard against the wall.

My free hand — the other still clutched the candlestick — wandered shamelessly, visiting all the places I'd touched in my fantasies that day. His chest. His rear. His groin...

Tuck hissed and lowered his head to my shoulder, breathing hard.

Hard, indeed, my animal side chuckled.

Unicorns were generally prim, old-fashioned souls, more apt to spout romantic poetry than actually getting it on. But my human side knew what I wanted and how to get it, so...

I slid my hand slowly over his shaft.

Tuck gasped, then locked a hand over mine. "We can't."

Oh yes, we could. I said so. Wasn't that enough?

"Come in," I whispered, pushing my bedroom door open with a foot.

His lips moved a few times before he spoke. "I can't."

I nearly laughed. Judging by the straining package in my hand, he could *come* in more ways than one.

"Of course you can." I slid my hand again.

He closed his eyes and gritted his teeth. "I shouldn't."

That's what he said. But his grip went from stopping my hand to guiding it. I grinned, following his lead, moving slowly up and down.

"Poor little monk needs some relief," I teased.

"Big monk," he grumbled.

I chuckled, letting my lips brush his ear. "You want this. I want this."

"I want a lot of things, but..."

Somewhere down the hall, something scuffed, and we froze. Then we relaxed. Just a cat — and not the extra-large one I wanted in my bed.

"Marian," he started in a *Try to be reasonable tone* he was probably more used to hearing than using. "I'm already bound for hell. But you..."

I laughed. "Arthur Richardson helped me get over that hurdle when I was seventeen."

"Arthur who?" he growled in a completely different tone.

My laugh carried down the dark hall. "Arthur Richardson, the blacksmith's son. Big hands, big body..." I smiled at the sweet memories. "He was just as clueless as I was back then, but we learned fast. Then there was George, the carpenter's boy. Lovely lad, and when it came to using his tools—"

Tuck groaned and thumped his head against the wall. "Too much information."

I laughed. "Sorry to tease, but you see my point?"

He grimaced. "About big hands and tools?"

I shook my head. "That was just fun and games, but even then, I knew something that feels so good can't be bad. And being with you... It's like we were meant to be together. How can that be wrong?"

"It is good," he murmured, holding me close. "Like a dream. But—"

I cut him off, shaking my head. "Tonight, no *buts*. Tonight, we get to do anything we want. We can *be* anyone we want." I smiled, touching his lips. "Like a brave knight getting his just reward from a lady whose eye he caught."

His eyes sparkled, and he glanced down at his groin. "More like, she caught me."

I laughed too loudly, then pulled him into my room. "See? Another reason to come in. Noise."

And, whoosh — the fire in his eyes flared.

"Noise, huh?"

I nodded, tugging him toward the bed. "Noise control, plus, this candle is going to be a fire hazard if I'm not careful. And I have no plans to be careful tonight."

"Are you saying this is all part of a dastardly plan?"

Ha. I was making this up as I went along, but it was nice that he thought me capable of engineering an escape, rallying loyal allies, and laying plans for a steamy night, all at the same time.

"I'm good at multitasking," I bluffed. "Now, don't move, unless it's to take off that robe. I need a moment."

With that, I lit the candles on the near side of the bed, then circled around to do the same on the far side. Each caught with a faint sizzle, then glowed restlessly, much like me. Placing the candlestick among them, I locked eyes with Tuck. Between us was the bed, the last physical obstacle other than our clothes.

I raised my hands to my collar and started unlacing my dress.

Across the bed, Tuck's breath hitched. Slowly, he moved his hands to his belt.

Still, he hesitated. "Marian..."

I shook my head firmly. "Forget about sin. This is destiny."

My throat went dry with a thought I didn't dare voice. One that said, *This might be our last chance.*

Tuck's face went hard in that ready-for-battle look. Then he sucked in a breath and pulled off his belt. "You're right."

I flashed him a saucy smile. "I'm always right. At least, that's what I'll pretend tonight."

He laughed, though it faded as I pushed my dress off my shoulders. Anticipation laced the air, and my pulse raced.

Still, I jutted my chin at him in a signal, keeping things fun.

"Oh, right," he said, throwing off his robe.

Too bad he wore a tunic under that. A tunic with an unmistakable tent at the front.

He gulped, waiting. "Your turn."

Candlelight swayed, and my body burned with need.

"My turn," I agreed, letting the dress pool at my feet.

Sadly, I had a chemise under that, but my deft fingers made quick work of that. Which left me with just the long length of cloth wrapped around my breasts.

Tuck stared, his mouth open a crack. Then he gave himself a little shake and asked, "Can I help with that?"

"If I can help with those." I grinned, indicating his breeches.

Cold air nipped at my skin as I circled the bed, but I knew that wouldn't last long. Tuck met me at the foot of the bed, where I raised my arms.

"Be my guest."

Without a word, he held the cloth as I turned in slow, sensual circles. Dancing, almost, in his arms.

When the last section of cloth fell away, the cold made my nipples peak. Well, maybe not just the cold.

His breeches followed that cloth to the floor, and I raised his hands to my chest.

"Tonight, dear knight, this maiden is all yours."

Chapter Fourteen

TUCK

Up to the time Marian took my hands, a thousand emotions battled for my soul. But the moment I touched her soft skin, all I felt was desire.

One minute, we were standing there, getting acquainted in the best possible way. The next, we were on the bed, intertwined.

"Tuck..." Marian whispered exactly the way she had in my dreams.

I inhaled her breast — or tried to, massaging the tip with my tongue. I traced her curves, marveling at her smooth, creamy skin, from her chest to her belly, then her legs...

Her hands slid purposefully down my rear, pressing me close. She wound her legs around me, opening to my touch. And touch I did, circling with my hand.

"Yes," she moaned, throwing her head back.

If this was the road to eternal damnation, I was all in.

Our hands and tongues tangled, while our words collided in midair. The dancing candlelight became a blur, and my body burned.

And yet, despite our heady rush, everything fell perfectly into place. Our bodies lined up all by themselves, and before I knew it, I slid home. In a stranger's bed, in a stranger's castle, in a place far, far from my childhood manor and the abbey — and yet I'd never felt more sure of home.

She was home.

Marian moaned, clutching my back. "Yes..."

We were a perfect fit, like a sword and its sheath. I knew, because I slid back and forth, testing the tailored fit. Then Marian squeezed her inner muscles around me, and I groaned in raw need.

"Two can play at that game, you know," I croaked, picking up the pace.

Her grin twisted in ecstasy, and she chuckled. "Oh, I know."

The faster I moved, the harder she squeezed — the very best kind of competition we were both bound to win. Our cries grew louder, making me grateful for the thick stone walls.

"Yes..." Marian panted, raising her arms over her head.

I pinned them there and withdrew to the very tip of my shaft. Then, at a nod from Marian, I hammered back in.

Marian bucked under me, urging me on. Straining in a way that told me neither Arthur nor George had come close to bringing her to this point. Just as no woman had ever pushed me to the edge I was teetering on now, about to explode.

Then I did, and she did, and all I could do was roar. Inside. Outside. My lion side, too. Light blasted all around me, and fire raced through my veins.

My lion growled, and my fangs pushed perilously close to the surface.

"Yes," Marian urged. "Now. Bite. Deep."

She arched her neck, giving me space. Nothing had ever tempted me more, but something held me back. Not rules in a book or warnings from a priest, but a sense of preserving that special moment for a better time and place.

"What could be better than now?" Marian grumbled, pressing me close.

I couldn't explain in words, so I pushed images into her mind instead. Images of peaceful places and happy people... Surroundings we could sneak away from to bond with a clear conscience, when the whole world was in harmony, not just us two.

She sighed, then slowly slumped. "You're right."

We held each other, still panting, still high on the magic of love. Then I closed my eyes and lay back. Marian nestled over me, her head on my shoulder, her hand on my chest. With a sigh, she circled a finger over my heart.

"A lion and a unicorn..."

I chuckled. "Maybe we'll be memorialized on a tapestry someday."

She laughed. "I would fill a hall with them. Every wall covered in a different scene." Her smile lasted a moment, then slowly faded, and she whispered, "Not hunting, I mean. Only happy scenes."

I nodded slowly, fighting to keep reality at bay. "Flowers...birds...banners flying in a breeze..."

Her chin bobbed. "Like the Garden of Eden."

I flashed a tight smile. "Without any serpents."

A minute passed as we clung to imaginary scenes I feared we would never see. All that time, Marian traced circles onto my chest.

"I've always wondered about mating bites," she whispered a little sadly.

I held her even closer. "I would teach you everything about them in a heartbeat. But as much as I hate waiting, we're in too much of a mess to truly enjoy it now." Then I tried a little joke. "Besides, imagine the uproar. Get it? Up-roar?"

She rolled her eyes, but I caught the smile she hid. "Well, let them roar. A lion and a unicorn can do whatever they damn well please."

I raised an eyebrow. "What about a priest and a noblewoman?"

She shook her head. "You're a knight, at least in your heart."

The words warmed me. Still, I knew the reality.

"Too bad wishing doesn't matter."

She lifted her head, scolding me. "It does matter. Well, maybe not wishing by itself. But wishing *and* planning *and* working hard at something — that can get you far. Look at me."

I grinned, letting my eyes feast on her bare body. "As you wish, m'lady."

She play-smacked me. "I mean, figuratively. I always wanted to be more than a proper lady. And here I am, plotting to save the country." She sighed. "Trying to, anyway."

I kissed her knuckles. "Succeeding. I'm sure of it."

She didn't look so sure, and frankly, it was a bit of a stretch for me too. Not because I lacked faith in her, but for the sheer enormity of the task.

"Not settling for being a proper lady, at least," she muttered, looking fierce. "And definitely not basking in my beauty."

I laughed. "You could be the most beautiful woman in the land and I wouldn't look twice, because that's not what I love about you."

She stared, and I nearly said, *oops*. She *was* the most beautiful woman in the land.

Candlelight bounced off her dark hair, emphasizing the point. Her soft, perfect features shone with the afterglow of sex, and her full lips moved.

Funny how all that had slipped my mind. For a moment, I felt like a fool. How could I forget?

But that was exactly the point. I loved Marian for so much more than all that.

"I mean, you're not bad..." I joked.

Her smile grew, saying *That's what I love about you. Among other things.*

Quiet, happy seconds ticked by as her eyes shone at me.

"Love, huh?"

I held her closer. "Love. So, watch out. I might still go for that mating bite."

There was so much darkness in the world, but her laughter peppered that with pinpoints of light.

"I hope you do."

I stroked her shoulder. "What do unicorns do?"

She flapped a hand vaguely. "Oh, you know. We prance around daintily, acting noble and showing off our natural beauty..."

For a minute, she had me. Then I burst out laughing. "Very funny. I mean, how do unicorns bond as mates?"

"Patience, good sir. I was getting to that."

Sticking an elbow on the mattress, she propped her head against one hand. With the other, she went back to circling my chest.

I was about to joke, but she went all serious, murmuring, "Close your eyes."

I watched her for a moment, then obeyed.

Around and around, her finger went, her soft touch arousing me all over again.

"Unicorns don't bite, but they do leave their mark," she whispered, nestling closer.

Her legs pressed against mine, and I held my breath, wondering what came next.

"Leave their mark...where?" I asked.

And dammit, my cock twitched.

She chuckled, but that didn't break the dreamy state I felt myself slipping into.

"Oh, we're far too proper for something crude," she teased, brushing her hand against my hip.

I gritted my teeth as my shaft swelled.

"No, we unicorns aim for where it counts most." Her tone was half lullaby, half seductress. "The heart."

Having my eyes closed meant every other sense piqued, and I imagined my heart swelling into the circle she traced.

"And what exactly do they aim with?" I asked.

She kissed my chest, following the path of her finger, giving nothing away.

"Help," I finally said. "I'm imagining a unicorn piercing my heart, and it's not poetic. Just bloody."

"Well, as a matter of fact..."

When I tensed, she laughed. "Not literally, I mean. Figuratively."

My brow furrowed as I tried to puzzle that out.

"Shh," she whispered, pressing me back. "Just relax."

"*Just relax, pierce,* and *horn* don't go together," I mumbled, but I did my best to obey.

Bit by bit, sounds and images wandered through my mind. A lush green meadow in summer. The sound of hoofbeats. Two horses — no, unicorns — frolicking in deep grass, rubbing noses and necks. . .

I had no idea what she was getting at, but it was strangely arousing.

Then again, I'd spent the last seven months locked up in a monastery, so it didn't take much to accomplish that.

Marian kissed my chest. "Soon. But first. . ."

The circles she traced spiraled inward, growing smaller until her finger caressed a single spot over my heart.

My pulse raced, and I felt the pressure inside — in a good way. Not so much a unicorn horn piercing my heart like a sword, but rather, pinning my soul to hers. Stitching our life-lines together. Making us one that would never, ever part.

Her touch remained gentle, but I felt something shift within me. My breath grew faster, and I put my hand over hers, praying she wouldn't stop. Marian's heart beat harder, too — I could feel it pound against my skin.

Little lightning bolts electrified my heart, and my chest heaved. I felt bigger, stronger. Suspended by a force outside my own.

"Lions bite," Marian whispered between kisses. "Unicorns bond at the heart."

And, wow. I could feel it. My body was a blade being engraved with a distinct new pattern.

Her kisses grew longer, deeper, and the tug on my heart increased. With a growly little moan, she straddled me. Then she jammed her hips over mine, all without breaking the kiss.

I kept her palm pressed to my heart with one hand and caressed her breast with the other, my mind in a spin. Then she pressed down, taking me in inch by inch.

If I hadn't been so breathless, I might have roared. But I could only move my lips in silent ecstasy as she rode me. Harder. Faster. Deeper.

Men talked, and I thought I'd heard it all — all the kinky little tricks, positions, and toys some folks liked to use. But, hell. I'd never imagined anything more erotic than what her finger and body were doing to me now.

"Tuck," she breathed again and again.

I pushed up when she pushed down. I slid my free hand to her perfect rear, keeping our bodies jammed tight. I cracked my eyes open, soaking in the sight of her coming undone.

"Don't stop," I whispered through locked teeth, afraid that coming now would break the magic spell.

"Never..." She moaned, throwing her head back.

With a long, sharp cry, she came, triggering my own release. We shuddered and held on to each other, awash in pure pleasure that went on and on.

Marian moaned with an aftershock, then slowly slumped over me. Her hand went flat, mirroring the way her body came to rest over mine. Still, that feeling of togetherness remained.

"That's the idea," she murmured into my shoulder. "To be united through thick and thin."

Minutes later, I mumbled in awe.

"What?" she asked, raising her head.

"And I thought unicorns were the best-kept secret in the land..."

She laughed. "We're not?"

I shook my head. "That's topped by sex with a unicorn."

Her smile was a burst of sunlight in my muddled brain. "Ah, how little you know."

My eyes went wide. "If you have some other unicorn tricks to share, I'm all ears." Then I glanced down. "Or all, er...other things."

She play-smacked me.

"I'll be sure to let you know. And that wasn't ordinary sex with a unicorn shifter..."

There she went again, mixing words that didn't: *ordinary, sex,* and *unicorn.* Or did she think I got around more than I did?

"...it was *bonding* with a unicorn." Her tone underlined the gravity of the occasion.

"You mean Arthur and George didn't get that treatment?"

She shook her head. "Absolutely not. I've never tried it before, actually." She nuzzled my cheek. "And I never will — except with you, dear knight."

I held her long and tight, fighting away the outside world. The next day was bound to bring an unexpected shitstorm or two, but that wouldn't stop me from cherishing every minute of this night. I let go of the bad, allowing my mind to wander only in a world of good.

Then I laughed — and laughed.

"What now?" Marian demanded.

"Just wait until I tell Cyril," I barely got out between sidesplitting hoots.

"Tell *whom*?" Her tone threatened me with a thousand painful deaths if I ever told anyone.

I collected myself long enough to explain. "Just joking. But, still. Picture Cyril — the one who draws dirty things in the margins of books — finding out about unicorn bonding."

Marian's laughter joined mine. "Please, no. He'll get it all wrong and draw us doggy-style."

I waggled my eyebrows. "Now there's an idea."

She turned in the scoop of my arms and wiggled her rear. "Not just an idea, my dear knight. More like a promise."

I grinned from ear to ear. The woman could wield a sword and a dagger. She could set booby traps. She could gallop through an entire night without tiring on her own four feet. And she knew what she wanted in bed, too?

When I pinched her arm, she squeaked. "What's that for?"

"Just checking if you're real or a fantasy."

She wiggled her rear again. "I'm quite sure I'm real. But there's only one way to find out." Then she laughed. "Actually, there are quite a few ways..."

My lion roared in glee, and my little — er, big — monk twitched against her hip.

"We might have to test them all," I warned.

Her sultry laugh was music to my soul. "I'm in if you're in, my good knight. I'm all in."

Chapter Fifteen

MARIAN

Given all the danger and intrigue I knew the day would bring, it really wasn't the kind of morning to lounge around.

But boy, did I lounge... and lounge... and lounge, with Tuck's help, of course.

We lounged on the bed. We lounged against the wall. We lounged on the rug by the fireplace, just like I'd dreamed.

We were still there, limbs intertwined, faces close. Then Tuck started kissing his way down my collarbone toward my breast.

I chuckled, twirling a finger in his unkempt hair. "You, dear friar, were born for trouble."

Undeterred, he continued his sensual mission.

"Hmm. Born for some other things too," he murmured, kissing his way around a nipple.

I arched, biting back another cry.

"Besides," he mumbled out of the side of his mouth. "You know what they say about trouble and trouble's mate..."

I giggled, then pressed him back in place. The last thing I wanted was to distract him now.

Then a knock sounded on the door, and we froze.

Well, Tuck froze. I was so heated up by then, my temperature merely dropped to *inferno* level.

"Dammit..." Tuck muttered.

We both knew the outside world would demand our attention soon. But still... now?

Another knock.

Tuck sulked. "If it's the devil coming to drag me to hell, he can wait."

I nuzzled his face. "None of that now."

We'd covered that topic several times. Theoretically, we might qualify for hell and damnation. Still, I had a hard time believing that. Two average peasants could fall in love and call it a common-law marriage. Why couldn't we?

It was the *monk* part that was the catch. Oh, and the *noble maiden* thing. Also...unicorn. We were supposed to marry well, and a lion shifter/monk would never do, no matter how well he did me.

I hid a grin at that dirty joke. Obviously, Tuck was rubbing off on me.

"M'lady..." someone called from the other side of the door.

Tuck pulled the sheet over our heads. "Pretend we're not here."

I giggled. If only hiding from the world were that easy.

"You are called to breakfast, m'lady," Jacobs, the Winthrops' butler, called outside.

"Tell him you're not hungry," Tuck whispered.

"M'lady, you are *most urgently* called to breakfast."

I frowned. Jacobs's voice was always calm and measured. *Always.* But now...

Tuck caught the hint too. With a quick kiss, he rolled away, grabbed a decorative sword from the wall, and hid behind the door. As soon as I had my robe tied and my hair patted down, I cracked the door open.

"Apologies, Jacobs."

When the servant bowed, a drop of sweat fell from his forehead to the floor. And when he stood again, his eyes telegraphed *Danger! Danger!*

I tilted my head toward the back stairs, watching Jacobs carefully.

He shook his head, barely perceptibly, and motioned the other way. "Lady Winthrop will meet you in the great hall."

The Winthrops were my father's oldest, steadiest friends, and Jacobs was their oldest, most loyal staff member. I trusted him implicitly. But something was clearly wrong.

I pulled a dagger from up my sleeve, showing it to Jacobs.

His throat bobbed, and he nodded. "Yes, m'lady. Informal dress would be fine."

My heart pounded, though I made sure to keep my voice light.

"Thank you, Jacobs. Please tell Lady Winthrop I'll be right there."

The moment I closed the door, Tuck and I both pressed against it, listening.

"Only Jacobs?" I whispered.

Tuck flared his nostrils. "Jacobs and two others. Humans." He shook his head. "I don't like this. Let's get out of here."

What was to like? But I had no choice.

"I'm needed in the great hall. Jacobs signaled as much."

"What if Jacobs is another traitor?"

"If we can't trust him, we can't trust anyone."

Tuck made a face. "I vote for not trusting anyone."

It took some persuading, but Tuck finally gave in. I dressed quickly, concealing weapons as I went. Tuck pulled on his tunic, strapped the sword over it, and threw his monk's robe over that.

"How do I look?"

I chuckled. "Like a knight hiding in a monk's robe. But the sword doesn't show, if that's what you mean."

We threw together a quick plan, then kissed. A kiss I yearned to hold for a long, long time. But today wasn't that day, and I knew it. Today was the day that could decide not just my future, but the future of the entire land.

I left the room first, eyeing every tapestry and every niche in the hall for hidden foes, but I saw no one.

No one in the hall, I called to Tuck in my mind.

Before last night, I'd had to strain to do so. But unicorn bonds were sacred, and now, it felt as if he were right by my side.

Be careful. His reply sounded clear as a bell in my mind.

I sensed him prowling down the hall behind me, though he made no sound. My skin tingled, knowing there was a lion back there. *My* lion.

That, at least, made me smile.

A smile that faded the moment I entered the great hall.

Guards stood in each corner of the room, not bothering to hide their swords. Lady Winthrop sat in her usual spot, but her back was as stiff as a pole. Her eyes met mine, then bounced back to the man slouched lazily in Lord Winthrop's chair.

My step hitched. Prince John?

Behind me, the huge double doors closed with a bang.

"Ah, the fair Maid Marian," Prince John called.

Ignoring him, I walked directly to the lady of the house, bowed, and took her hand. "Good morning, m'lady."

"Good morning, my dear." She forced a tight smile.

"And Lord Winthrop... is he well?" I ventured.

Prince John cackled. "He is... for now."

I turned, making sure my eyes didn't drift to the chapel on the right, then forced myself to dip into a teensy, tiny bow. That was the prince, after all.

I'd met him several times, and every time, I was reminded of his brother, the king. They had the same boxy beard, the same V-shaped eyebrows, the same strong nose. All in all, the prince was a lot like Richard — but less in every way. Less tall. Less commanding. Less handsome. Less knightly, if there was such a thing.

On the other hand, he scored much higher on other scales — those that measured greed, selfishness, and cruelty.

I bristled. "What do you mean, Lord Winthrop is well *for now*?"

Prince John burst out laughing. "My dear Marian, straight to business, as always."

I formed my hands into fists, barely holding back that I was neither *his* nor *dear*.

"Women should concentrate on what they were born for," the prince lectured. "Business is neither fitting nor becoming of the fair sex — even a woman as ravishing as you."

My hackles rose at *fair sex*, but *ravishing* sent ice sliding down my spine.

I faked a bored sigh. "Well, you know how it is. It's all work, work, work for those of us who serve our country, especially in the absence of our beloved king."

His eyes flashed, but before he could spit whatever poison formed on his tongue, the guard in the nearest corner drew his sword and threw open the chapel door.

"You there!" he boomed.

My heart leaped when I spotted Tuck there, ready to fight. Thank goodness for Lady Winthrop's quick wits.

"Don't you dare enter my private chapel!" she admonished the guard. "And don't you dare interrupt a man of God going about his holy mission!"

The guard looked doubtful, because other than the clothes, Tuck was all knight. But the prince couldn't see Tuck from where he was seated, and he waved the guard down.

"Leave him. Besides, Lord Winthrop might be in need of his services soon. One last time."

I glared.

The guard slid the door shut, but it rolled back a few inches. I couldn't see much of the chapel, but that sliver was enough for Tuck to peer at us. I heard the pew creak as he knelt, pretending to pray.

Prince John's eyes crawled over every inch of my body, and he flashed a lecherous smile.

"You know, I was tempted to surprise you last night. But I suppose that wouldn't be seemly. Not for a future queen. And not until our wedding night."

Ugh. The man disgusted me. But, yikes. I'd never been more glad to be a unicorn. Our natural scent was a faint, flowery aroma that didn't absorb well. So, no garlic smells to worry about, no body odor...no giveaway scent of lion or sex either. Whew.

"Future queen?" I called him out on that. "That would be the king's bride, whomever he chooses."

"Exactly." Prince John kept his eyes level on me, making his plans clear.

I played dumb, the way he preferred his women. "But until the king returns..."

"From prison? From the Crusades?" He snorted, reached for a sweet roll, and started buttering it with crude swipes of a huge knife. "So many dangers he faces. So many enemies."

Starting with you, I wanted to hiss.

"Anything can happen," the prince went on. "We must be prepared to serve in his place."

You mean, serve yourself, I burned to say.

But antagonizing him wouldn't help, so I kept my mouth shut.

The prince shoved half the roll in his mouth and kept talking, revealing the gooey mess with every slurred syllable.

"Yes, the most unexpected things can happen. The way I received your message to meet here."

"How very interesting. I sent no such message. As a prince, you must be on guard against traitors at all times," I scolded.

There. Two could play at that game of speaking between the lines.

"Oh, believe me, I am." He stuck the remainder of his roll into his mouth, showing a hint of his wolf fangs, and started buttering another.

I'd never seen him in wolf form, but I knew he was a shifter. The man reeked of it.

Most shifters had a telltale scent — not unicorns, but we were exceptions in so many ways — a subtle one that reflected how they spent time in animal form. That meant most shifters smelled of fresh air, the forest, or open glens.

The prince smelled of schemes and intrigue. An unmistakably foul, musty scent.

"Which reminds me..."

He tortured me with an ominous pause. What would he threaten me with next?

"...the taxes I sent my men to collect — regretfully, of course. We must set an example for the people, you know."

Ha. I had him there. "I sent you enough treasure to cover those taxes, as instructed. It's not my fault it was stolen."

Actually, it was, but if he could lie, so could I.

"By Robin Hood and his bandits," he muttered.

Her bandits, I itched to correct him.

"I can only hope your brother, the king, returns soon to restore order to the land," I said primly.

"One can only hope," he said with no sincerity whatsoever. "I worry about him, you know."

Oh, I bet he did.

"And I worry about you, dearest betrothed," he went on.

I folded my arms. "We are not betrothed. You do not have my father's permission."

He frowned. "No, not yet. But seeing as he has been gone for so long..."

I bristled. My father had left over a year ago to try to persuade the king his country needed him at home. I'd last seen my father when he'd visited briefly, six months earlier — just long enough to spread the word of Richard's capture and get the ball rolling in terms of collecting the required ransom. Then he'd returned to the continent to make sure our monarch was being treated properly, even in prison.

"If an ill fate were to befall him..." John hinted.

I stuck up my chin. "If anything befalls my father, my cousin becomes my guardian."

Since I was a woman and an only child, my father's title and holdings would go to my cousin, Thomas, whom I trusted implicitly.

John cracked an egg open. "And if an ill fate were to befall him?"

I showed my teeth. God, what a snake this man was.

"Then my godfather would become my guardian," I snipped.

I didn't add what he already knew — the king was my godfather.

"Yes, but if anything were to happen to him..." Prince John's smug grin cut to my soul. "Fear not, dear lady. I will do my duty and take over the guardianship. In fact, I already have."

I stalked closer, looming over his chair. So close, I could hear the creak of armor as his guards stepped closer. I growled, enunciating each word.

"You are not my guardian. You never will be."

And damn the man, who smiled ever more smugly.

"Ah, but I am." He waved the egg. "These are difficult times, with so many men away at the Crusades. Therefore, I have passed a decree to protect young ladies of noble blood in the absence of their menfolk. There are just too many irreputable men lurking about, looking to take advantage of their wealth."

"Oh, I know," I snarled, barely holding back, *Men like you, you scheming prick.*

He nodded, clearly pleased with his own genius. "Exactly. I only have your best interests at heart. Besides, what woman wouldn't want to marry a king?"

"Prince, you mean."

"Prince. For now," he grumbled. He took a bite of his egg, then held the rest up to me.

It took everything I had not to smack his hand away or, better yet, punch his arrogant mug.

"You're overwhelmed, I can see." His voice went all condescending. "Perfectly natural, considering how near the big day draws." His eyes glinted. "The feast of Saint Matthias."

"Three days away," I reminded him. Not that that gave me much time.

He shook his head. "We shall marry on the eve of the feast of Saint Matthias. Don't worry," he hurried to add, "all the arrangements are being made by a dear friend. She'll make sure everything is perfect. As a man, I have neither the time nor inclination for such things."

I growled, reminding him I felt the same way. Especially when it came to marriage to *him.*

"What friend?" I spat, one sharp syllable after another.

His smile stretched. "The lovely Lady Thornton. She's even found the perfect location — Nottingham."

I stared. Nottingham?

Up to that moment, Tuck had been mumbling nonsensical prayers in the chapel. Now, he went perfectly still, like me.

There was no missing it — that sense of pawns being maneuvered around a chessboard by a cruel, calculating hand. And while Prince John was both those things, checkers was more his game. Chess demanded a mastermind. Which meant. . .

Lady Thornton?

That bitch? Tuck's voice broke into my mind.

She was the only one capable of ticking all three boxes: cruel, conniving, and a mastermind.

I stared at the prince, whose smug smile told me he had no clue. Whatever Lady Thornton had planned would serve her and her alone.

"And if I refuse?" I barked, tired of tiptoeing around.

Prince John studied his knife. "Alas, there is no other option. Well, I suppose there is another. But you really, really don't want to explore that one."

I gave him my hardest *You don't scare me* look.

He tested the blade against his thumb and murmured, "Just think. . ."

Like I hadn't already been doing that.

"Think of the lovely gifts I would grant you," he continued.

"There's nothing you have that I desire." My tone made it clear I meant nothing. Especially *him*. "How dare you speak of gifts while threatening those I hold dear?"

"Such as?"

God, I could kill him just for that amused tone.

"Such as Lord Winthrop."

Prince John snorted. "What about that traitor?"

"Spare him."

"No, he must be made an example of."

"Spare him," I insisted.

"All right, then. I'll spare him as a wedding gift. You come along peacefully, and no tricks."

I hid my disdain. I wasn't supposed to use tricks, but the prince could whenever they suited his purpose? Not fair.

I glared, but what could I do?

The prince gleefully signaled his men. "Prepare my bride's carriage. We depart in ten minutes." Then he turned to me, shaking a finger. "And no tricks."

Ha. I already had my first one planned.

"No tricks," I lied. "But I must pray first."

Chapter Sixteen

TUCK

The minute Marian stalked into the chapel, I slid the door shut and grabbed her arm. I was getting her out of there, and that was that.

But booted feet stomped over, guarding each of the doors — one to the great hall, one to the corridor — complicating that plan.

Marian took my hand and kneeled, pretending to pray.

"You can't go with him," I whisper-hissed.

"I have no choice. He'll kill Lord Winthrop. Heck, he'll probably torch the entire town."

My hands clutched the pew before me so hard, it was a wonder it didn't break.

"So, we take him on right now and end this. You and I," I declared.

Marian rolled her eyes. "Take on the prince, his four guards, and the platoon waiting outside?"

Good point. But still...

Marian bowed her head, thinking aloud. "I've avoided him long enough. It's time to make my own move."

I stared. How was riding away with him her move?

"Let him think I'm playing along..." she whispered.

I made a face. "He's not stupid."

"No, but he needs me alive."

I scowled. "For now."

Plus, her life wasn't all he threatened. If he laid a hand on her...

She elbowed me. "Have you no faith in my ability to take care of myself?"

"I have full faith in you. But not even a giant can hold back a flood."

God, now I sounded like old Christopher, the oldest of the Merry Men, who was prone to spouting words of wisdom that didn't always make sense.

"You know what I mean," I finished a little lamely.

"We need to strike on territory where we have the upper hand," Marian mused.

I angled the sword I'd hidden under my robe, letting it prod her foot. "I can strike him right now."

"And be cut down by his men afterward?" She shook her head. "I want you alive, Friar."

She squeezed my hand, sending warmth through my soul. Warmth and wonder. What on earth did a goddess like her see in a man like me?

She snorted, reading my mind. "I see honor. Honesty. Love. A desire to serve. Oh, and the robe is kind of cute too."

I chuckled — quietly — and locked eyes with her.

Then my heart squeezed — really squeezed — and my eyes went wide in wonder.

Marian nodded, smiling. "And you thought I was kidding about the unicorn bond."

I'd thought no such thing, but wow. I could feel it now, illuminating my soul like the noon summer sun. It shone into every corner, finding pockets of strength, patience, and determination I didn't know I had.

I clasped her hand and blew out a long breath. The only thing I lacked was a plan.

But Marian, as usual, was ahead of me on that one.

"We have a better chance on the open road. I could kill him, then get away."

I stared. "How?"

"Well, a diversion would be good..." Then her eyes lit up.

"Oh no," I protested when I realized what she had in mind. "I am not leaving you."

"Yes, you are," she insisted. "Just long enough to race ahead and get Robynne's help. I'll delay the carriage."

"How?"

She grinned. "Unicorn tricks. I have many. Didn't you know?"

No, I didn't. And I didn't like this plan.

"Robynne will get word of this soon enough. I'll stay near you," I insisted.

She shook her head. "No, you won't. You'll speed ahead to Robynne and make a plan. A good plan," she emphasized. Then she chuckled. "Not that I'll be waiting for some random man to show up at the right place and time to save me."

I grinned at that echo of our meeting, what felt like a lifetime ago.

"No strings attached, of course," I whispered. "Only your hand in marriage and entrapment as my bedmate forever."

And oops. My voice went all breathy there.

Then I slumped. "Nice fantasy, huh?"

She leaned her head against mine. "Not a fantasy. A promise."

I held her hand tighter. "I swear." Then I caught myself. "Of course, there's usually one critical detail I overlook, so brace yourself. Something is bound to go wrong."

She chuckled. "Everything has already gone wrong, but some things have gone right. Like meeting you. Like last night. Like this." She indicated our clasped hands. "Besides, it's like Willa said. *The best things in life happen when you least expect them.*"

I sucked in a deep breath, trying to convince myself that was true.

Then footsteps stomped outside, and someone hammered on the door. "Enough praying. Time to depart."

My teeth extended, and the stubble on my chin thickened.

Time to kill that fool, my lion growled.

Marian rubbed her thumb over my hand. "Soon." She raised her voice to holler, "Coming!" then swooped in for a kiss.

I cupped her face, digging deep to find the strength to follow her crazy plan.

"A few minutes after we leave, find Lord Winthrop. Take his fastest horse and ride to Sherwood Forest," Marian whispered.

I nodded grimly. This felt more and more like my dreams of the Crusades — but Daniel was right. There was no thrill, no excitement. Just dread, because so much could go wrong, and so many could suffer.

Especially Marian, my lion fretted.

My stomach roiled at the horrible images that conjured up, but I fought them away. I had to focus if I was to protect the woman I loved.

"See you soon," she whispered, standing.

It took everything I had to remain kneeling. A handy position for the praying it would take to make this plan work.

"Soon," I whispered. "I promise."

∞∞∞∞

I did exactly as Marian said, with one added detail to console myself as her carriage clattered out the castle gate.

"You," I hissed, slamming a man against the wall.

A gasp went out, and Lord Winthrop, who'd just been freed by his men, barked.

"Unhand that man!"

I shook my head, squeezing the man's neck. "Do you pay your men in silver coins?"

Winthrop stared, confused. "No..."

With one hand, I kept the man pinned in place. With the other, I revealed the contents of his pockets — a handful of silver coins.

"You don't pay your men in silver coins, but Prince John does. I saw his guards paying off this traitor. He must have sent word to Prince John that Marian was here."

"But...Henry..." Winthrop sputtered.

I scoffed. A good reminder for me never to trust anyone. Well, no one but Marian. And Robynne.

Don't forget Willa and John, my lion chimed in.

Reluctantly, I added the sheriff to that list, because you didn't have to like a man to trust him.

And Alan and Martin and Rob— My lion stopped on the cusp of adding Robert. *Okay, maybe not Robert. But the others, yes.*

All in all, a pretty impressive list. An army, one might say. An army I would be proud to fight with.

I squeezed the traitor's neck, ready to finish him off. His feet were dangling above the ground by then, and his voice was a wheeze.

"You're a man of God. You can't kill."

Ha. If only he knew.

"I can kill the devil," I snarled, continuing to squeeze.

But one of Father Benjamin's sermons echoed through my mind just then. Something about mercy and turning cheeks...or was that the one about a serpent?

I wasn't really sure, because I rarely paid attention in church. But, still. I'd obviously picked up some trivia.

I didn't know whether to be proud of myself or aghast. But I did know one thing.

I had no more time to waste. Marian's life depended on it.

I threw the traitor to the ground and all but snapped my fingers at Winthrop.

"I need a horse. Now."

Never mind that he was a lord and I was a mere friar. The woman I loved was in danger, and I was in a rush.

His eyes bored into mine. Then he nodded and turned to Jacobs. "Do as he says."

Minutes later, I was thundering toward Sherwood Forest.

Chapter Seventeen

MARIAN

Well, Tuck was right about one thing: the part about things going wrong.

Prince John didn't ride in the carriage with me. He rode his own horse, giving me no opportunity to slit his throat.

Damn shame.

At least I had Lady Winthrop for company. She'd insisted on accompanying me, saying it wouldn't be proper for a young lady to travel without a chaperone. She kept a straight face at the time but winked the moment Prince John turned his back.

And boy, was I happy for the company.

When a breathless messenger came galloping up, my hopes rose for something — anything — to distract Prince John from marrying me, or to at least buy time. But the message, whatever it was, didn't have the effect I'd hoped for. Quite the opposite, in fact, because the mysterious news only made Prince John spur everyone on — literally.

"Move it," he snapped at his troops while pushing his own mount harder. "There's no time to waste."

Lady Winthrop and I looked at each other.

"Maybe our allies are finally on the move," she whispered.

My hopes peaked, then faded over the next few hours. No allies rushed to my aid, nor did helpful bandits appear. Just Lady Winthrop and me creaking along in that carriage.

Of course, I didn't sit idly. I worked with the horses to cause delay after delay. One stumbled, throwing his mount, the captain of the guard. Another skittered sideways into the horses hitched to the wagon, tangling the harness. Others whinnied, reared, and refused to go on. But I couldn't overuse such tricks, lest the soldiers grow too cruel in their reactions.

At noon, another messenger rode up, and that time, my hopes were even more cruelly dashed.

"Robin Hood has been captured!" the man cried as he passed the troops.

Prince John usually rode near the carriage, so I heard the whole breathless report.

"Robin Hood has been captured! He turned himself in at Nottingham!"

At that point, I'd shrugged, unconcerned. Robynne was a woman. They must have had the wrong person.

But then the messenger corrected himself. "Turned *herself* in, I mean."

"Robin Hood — a woman?" Prince John gasped, along with many others.

I rolled my eyes, and Lady Winthrop patted my hand. "Now, now. The more they think we're weak and incapable, the better our chances of delivering a sound surprise."

She was right, but still, I grumbled. "We're on the dawn of the twelfth century. How much longer will it take for men to appreciate what women are capable of?"

"By the time your children have children," Lady Winthrop told me. "I'm sure of it."

A quick estimate put that at about 1239. That long?

My gut said that was on the optimistic side, but heck. A girl could hope.

Or maybe I shouldn't, at least when it came to the part about children. How was that ever going to happen if the man I loved was a monk? We might have shared one sizzling night, but the moment Tuck took his vows, it would be bye-bye to any bang-bang for the two of us. And if I couldn't have Tuck, I didn't want anyone.

I cut off those thoughts before they pushed me even deeper into despair. The present was hard enough, especially if the real Robynne Hood had been caught.

I doubted it at first, but then I overheard Prince John mutter gleefully, "I knew I could count on Jessica."

My gut sank. Jessica was Lady Thornton, and this was exactly her type of trick. But why would Robynne turn herself in?

As it turned out, for the same reason I'd agreed to ride with Prince John. Blackmail.

I overheard it in snatches of conversation that rippled through the soldiers riding around us. Apparently, Lady Thornton, hell-bent on avenging her brother, had seized a young woman and her children in Nottingham's marketplace in broad daylight, such was her scorn for the law.

"Lady Thornton gave Robin Hood until this morning to turn himself in," one of the messengers said. "If he didn't, she threatened to kill a child every hour, and the mother, Bess, first."

My heart leaped. Bess? The sweet young woman I'd visited with Tuck on alms day?

If Lady Thornton had ridden up with the news herself, I would have pulled a dagger and gone at her, consequences be damned. What kind of monster did such a thing?

"Good thinking!" The prince nodded appreciatively, answering my unspoken question. A monster like my future husband — at least, he would be, if things continued in this vein.

"Robin Hood — a woman?" The men jabbered about that all afternoon.

Less wowed by the *woman* part, I pondered a different question. Why would Robynne surrender? She had to know Lady Thornton was not to be trusted. The Merry Men needed her leadership, and the people of Nottinghamshire needed her too. Why lay all of that on the line?

Lady Winthrop's eyes twinkled when I posed the question to her.

"Perhaps for the same reasons you are here now. Because there's someone you trust — intimately — to help enact a bold, last-minute plan."

I stared, but she just chuckled.

"Oh, I saw enough of you and that friar to catch on."

My jaw fell open. Tuck and I had spent no more than three minutes in the chapel that morning — behind a mostly closed door.

Lady Winthrop laughed. "I knew about thirty seconds after you two arrived last night, standing studiously apart. Then there was that glow you came to breakfast with..."

My cheeks heated, and I nearly protested. *Glow? What glow?*

She laughed harder. "I've never seen a priest look quite so satisfied, I can assure you."

My unicorn side pranced away with that thought, as inappropriate as it was. *Last night meant as much to him as it did to us. Tuck likes us! He loves us!*

Well, yes. But he was also a priest.

Didn't stop you from shagging him on every conceivable surface last night, my unicorn pointed out.

No, it hadn't. But that was destined to be our one and only night, and we both knew it. Our love was a condemned prisoner, permitted one last indulgence before it all came to an ugly end.

"Now, now. Don't look so glum," Lady Winthrop scolded. "You'll think of something."

I stared at her. How could she have such faith?

She took my hands in hers. "Dear child, you are your mother's daughter, and your father taught you well."

It wasn't often that I thought of my mother, who died when I was young — too young. Now that I did, tears sprang to my eyes and my heart swelled. Enough to make me realize another kind of unicorn bond existed there. She might be gone, but she would always be with me.

My throat grew thick. "I'm like her?"

My father had assured me of that a thousand times. But to hear it from someone else...

"You have the same drive, the same spunk. The same stubbornness," Lady Winthrop said.

I frowned. "I'm not stubborn."

She laughed. "You sound like her too." She squeezed my hands. "She was my dearest friend, and I knew her better than anyone. Maybe even better than your father, because we went back that far. So, yes. You're just like her. Right down to your choice in men."

My eyes went wide, though Lady Winthrop flapped her hand like it was obvious.

"Strong. Loyal. Loving. Not quite as sharp as you, but sharp enough to listen to you, and listen well."

"But...but..."

"But what, child?"

Um, where would I begin?

"He's a monk," I finally said.

She shrugged. "The Lord moves in mysterious ways." Then she leaned back and took a few deep breaths. "Enough of that. It's time to compose ourselves."

Sensing she might pull out her needlepoint, I nearly screamed. But she just sat back, closed her eyes, and murmured, "A good general uses the calm before the storm to think ahead. She takes stock of her forces. She considers every angle of attack — and retreat. She plans for every likely scenario, then for every unlikely, even impossible one."

I stared. "She?"

Lady Winthrop shot me a prim look. "My dear girl, you do know that my husband and your father fought in the Battle of Montgisard, all those years ago, when they were young?"

I nodded dumbly.

She chuckled, then dropped the bombshell. "Well, you don't think I let my husband go crusading alone, do you?" She tut-tutted, then leaned back again. "Now, as I said. Let us use the calm before the storm to prepare."

I stared, then followed suit. And bit by bit, hope filtered back into my soul. I had a hell of a lot of unlikely allies — Willa, Robynne, and, most of all, Tuck. But, wow. Maybe I'd just stumbled across one more.

Chapter Eighteen

TUCK

Galloping away from Marian was hell. Watching from a distance as Prince John, his men, and Marian's carriage passed through Nottingham's east gate by flickering torchlight had been hell.

And *hell* was what I vowed to rain down on Prince John and Lady Thornton as I galloped into Sherwood Forest on Snow not long afterward.

Yes, Snow — Marian's beautiful white mare. Lord Winthrop had given me his best horse, but it had already been ridden hard the previous day through all the messaging back and forth between allies. The horse ran gallantly, but after an hour, he pulled up lame.

I was about to shift and run on my own four feet when Snow appeared out of nowhere. At first, I'd wondered how she'd found me, but then I knew.

Thank you, Marian, I whispered, petting Snow.

I could feel our unicorn bond tug on my heart, directing me toward my mate. Marian must have passed the reverse information to Snow.

As I'd saddled her with the gear from my exhausted horse, Snow tossed her mane.

I'm only subjecting myself to this indignity for my mistress, you know.

Oh, I knew. And I appreciated it.

Thank you, Snow, I'd said as I mounted.

She shot off, as concerned for Marian as I was.

She'd reared and whinnied angrily when Marian's wagon entered Nottingham and only reluctantly turned for Sherwood Forest afterward. But she carried me as quickly and faithfully as I could ask, thundering through the forest.

And, *zing!* The metallic sound of a dozen hastily drawn swords greeted our approach to Robynne's camp.

"Halt! Who goes there?" John Little boomed.

"Watch out! It's a knight," Robert warned. "And boy, does he look angry."

Yes, I was. And as for the *knight* part...from now until the time I freed Marian, that was what I would be.

Funny how a man could yearn for something for years, only to find himself willing to trade his soul to reverse the situation completely. Being a knight was my sole desire, but not if it meant Marian was in danger.

My lion snarled. *When I get my claws on Prince John...*

Oh, we would make him pay, all right. We would definitely make him pay.

I leaped off Snow before she even stopped. Not a great move, because the momentum nearly propelled me into the bonfire. I took five huge, careening strides before I pulled up at the edge of the flames.

"Watch it there, son," old Christopher muttered.

I took a step back, gulping.

"Tuck?" John Little's eyes went wide.

"They have Marian," I blurted — at the very same time that Robert uttered almost those exact words.

"They have Robynne!"

I stared. "What?"

"Wait — they have Marian too?" Willa cried.

A moment of chaos ensued, and even then, I did a double take.

"Wait. What are you doing here?" I asked Willa and John.

"Long story," she muttered darkly. "You first."

Speaking so quickly I stumbled over my own words, I explained what had happened in Winthrop.

"Damn the king's scheming brother," John — the bear shifter, not the prince — growled.

"What about you two?" I asked. "What happened at the abbey?"

"The plan worked as far as the monks not realizing it was me, not Marian, in the library," Willa said. "But then a cohort of soldiers arrived to escort Marian to Nottingham."

"On whose orders?" I growled.

"Who else?" John muttered.

I bared my teeth. "Lady Thornton?"

Willa nodded glumly. "We had no choice but to fight our way out of there. They followed us into the woods, but once we shifted into bear form, they changed their minds — quickly." She flashed a little smile.

At least there was that — Willa and John were safe. But what about Robynne?

Then Willa's smile faded. "It never occurred to us what Lady Thornton would do next."

I shuddered to think what it might be. There was no limit to the ugly things that woman's mind was capable of.

Willa looked at John, then me. "Lady Thornton took Bess and her children as hostages. She threatened to kill one child every hour until Marian turned herself in."

The blood drained from my cheeks. Bess? The children?

Then I gulped. Had I unwittingly given Lady Thornton the idea?

They promised not to hurt anyone else if I cooperated... I'd told her that day she'd interrogated me in Nottingham.

Not a bad strategy, she'd mused.

I felt sick.

Of course, Marian would have surrendered herself immediately, even if it meant her own life. But seeing as Marian hadn't known...

Robert's voice cracked when he filled in the rest. "Robynne decided to turn herself in instead."

"She should have let me go in her place," John growled.

Willa touched his arm. "Her plan made sense. But now..."

When she trailed off, a deathly silence fell over the camp. Now, everything had gone wrong.

I cursed. "Why would Robynne turn herself in? She knows Lady Thornton can't be trusted."

"We worked out a plan." Willa pointed to a scratched map in the ground. "A solid one, with the sheriff as backup."

My hopes perked a little at that. "Lady Thornton still doesn't know he's a dragon — and that he's on our side?"

"We think not. So, Daniel was our backup plan." Then she made a face. "A plan that didn't call for Prince John marching into Nottingham with a hundred men."

"With a hundred men *and* Marian," I muttered bitterly.

"Then there's the fact that Lady Thornton didn't release Bess as promised," Willa added.

"You didn't see that coming?" I snarled, though my malice was aimed at my enemies, not my friends.

"We did, but Robynne was right," Willa said. "Even if that *Thornton bitch* — Robynne's words, not mine — released Bess and the children, she could easily snatch new hostages. At least this way, Robynne hoped to lull Lady Thornton into a false sense of security."

I curled my hands into near-claws. "Marian was thinking along the same lines, but I fear we may have underestimated our enemies."

Everyone stood in stunned silence, trying to digest it all.

Then, with a whoosh of air and a piercing cry, an eagle swooped into camp. It circled twice, then landed on the far side of the fire. The flames between us hid the details, but I saw the air shimmer as the bird gradually morphed into a man. The huge wings were the last part to shift, making the naked birdman before us a hell of a sight.

Willa grimaced and turned the other way. "The downside of living with a band of male shifters..."

The next time I blinked, it was just Alan a'Dale, shaking out his arms and peering at us with those piercing dark eyes.

"What news, Alan?" John demanded.

Someone threw him a cloak, and he pulled it on while stepping over. "I just flew over Nottingham. Word is, Robynne is to be executed tomorrow."

Everyone went totally, mournfully silent.

As Alan continued, the news only got bleaker. "Prince John has also announced that he will marry Marian the day after."

"The eve of the feast of Saint Matthias," I muttered.

Everyone waited, looking blank.

"Patron saint of carpenters, tailors, victims of smallpox," I added. "Matthias replaced Judas as one of Christ's apostles."

Everyone looked at me as if I were a raving lunatic — or an overzealous clergyman. Everyone but Willa, who stared. "You mean, the way Prince John wants to replace King Richard?"

"That's what Marian suspects." I nodded, then snarled. "If he touches her, I'll kill him. I swear, I will tear that man limb from limb."

Everyone stared. Then their glances softened, and old Christopher murmured wistfully, "Ah, love."

All of them quickly caught on to the fact that their local friar was in love with a noblewoman he had no hope of ever marrying. All except Robert.

"In love? Who?" he asked, looking around.

Willa rolled her eyes. "Forget it."

The men shot me sidelong glances and whispered their surprise to one another.

I glared into the fire, not caring that my secret was out. What did it matter? I could never have Marian. The best I could hope for was to help her get out of this alive so she could go on to live happily ever after with some other man.

My heart bled at the notion, but there was no other way. And since I couldn't bear to witness that...

I took a deep breath. Then I would die nobly in combat.

All around me, the Merry Men jabbered, tossing out ideas for salvaging a desperate situation. I ought to have felt just as overwhelmed, but calm settled over me, making everything suddenly, eerily clear.

I could see it all play out before me. I would fight boldly, bravely. I would save Marian.

And I would die.

All so hauntingly simple, and somehow comforting.

Maybe this was how knights felt on the eve of battle.

Then I corrected myself with a little smile. Marian could save herself, but I would lay the groundwork for her to fight her way out of Nottingham. I would fight at her side, and when the make-or-break moment arrived, I would take it.

I grinned, realizing that was my ace. Having made up my mind to die, I had an edge over every other soldier on the battlefield. Whether it was a flying arrow or a swinging sword that rushed at me, I wouldn't think like a person who hoped to survive. I would take it, gladly, as long it ensured survival for the woman I loved.

And, hey. Maybe the Merry Men would sing songs about me someday. Maybe every year on the anniversary of the eve of Saint Matthias, Marian would shed a few tears and light a candle for me.

A lump formed in my throat at that one, but I suppose that came with *brave knight* territory. For the remaining eighteen hours of my life — plus or, more likely, minus — I could cast the frustrated monk aside and bask in the bold, bright light filling my soul now.

"Uh, Tuck?" someone elbowed me.

I blinked and found John studying me quietly. Too quietly, with pinched lips that said he knew where my calm had come from.

Then he gripped my arm — hard, like a man tugging a stubborn mule in the opposite direction — and murmured, "There's always a way."

If he meant hope, I had plenty. But only for Marian.

"And it all starts with a solid plan," John continued.

I nodded cheerily, because I already had one.

He shook his head slightly. "A plan made by someone much, much smarter than you or me."

I frowned at that, because Robynne wasn't here to counsel us. Neither was Marian.

John waggled his eyebrows and slid his eyes to Willa.

At that exact moment, she stuck up her hands and hollered, "Quiet, everyone! I'm thinking."

A hush fell over the men, and even a full minute later, when Robert scratched his head and murmured something, the men elbowed him.

"Shush! She's thinking!"

Even the dogs leaned in, watching Willa sketch on the ground slowly, then faster. And faster still, until we could practically cup the anticipation in the air with our hands and hold it.

Even then, Willa kept her head down and that stick steadily moving. Nosewise sat at her feet, drooling in reverent silence.

It was only many minutes later that Willa stepped back, considered the sketch, and nodded to herself. Then she took a deep breath and motioned everyone closer.

"All right, everyone. Here's the plan. Listen closely."

We did, and I had to hand it to her. It was brilliant.

Step by step, she worked her way through it as if looking through time and telling a story backward.

"In order to free Robynne, we have to do this... And for that to happen, we have to set this up first..." Willa's voice rose and fell.

Never, ever had the Merry Men listened so intently.

She went on in that vein for a while, then took a deep breath and concluded.

"And for all that to happen, we need to start with one thing. The choir of Winslow Abbey."

My hopes sank like a stone, and I raised a hand sadly. "Just one catch. There is no choir at Winslow Abbey."

Willa didn't so much as blink an eye. She just grinned. "There is now. Or at least, there will be."

Chapter Nineteen

MARIAN

"Sleep well, my bride?" Prince John asked through the bars of my cell.

I flashed a sunny smile. "Indeed, I did. So many happy dreams." I let a heartbeat go by before following up with the punch line. "I dreamed a thousand different versions of your death." I stretched my arms high in an exaggerated yawn. "The kind of dream you enjoy so much, you never want them to end. But when you remind yourself how dreams can spill over into real life... All in all, a lovely way to start the day."

His dark eyes flashed. "Watch what you say to your future king."

I fluttered my eyelashes. "You mean, our dear Richard when he returns?"

I swear, the prince would have gone for my throat the moment a guard opened the cell door. Happily, Lady Winthrop launched herself between us first.

"Ah, it's you again. Good morning." She smiled at the prince as if it were any normal day, then motioned to the guard. "Two teas, please. One with a spot of milk, one without."

Which only riled Prince John further.

"There will be no tea! It's execution time." He leaned in, exhaling garlicky breath in my face. "And no tricks. I'll be watching you closely, and so will my guards. Any sign of trouble, and we'll kill the children."

The ultimate bargaining chip, and he knew it. Bess and her children had been locked up somewhere nearby, and I'd heard them sob all night. All but her eldest, Tom, whose efforts to cheer his mother broke my heart.

"It will be all right, Mummy. A brave knight will save us."

I gulped, thinking of Tuck. Had Snow found him? Had he reached the Merry Men? Was all lost, or was Tom right?

My fingers itched, tempted to knife Prince John on the spot. I had several blades stashed in my dress, so the knife part was easy. But that would only eliminate one danger, leaving Lady Thornton free to kill Robynne and the hostages.

Lady Winthrop and I had gone through all the options the previous night, and she was right. Our best hope was to launch a coordinated attack outdoors, where innocents like Bess had a better chance of fleeing.

Coordinated meant me, Lady Winthrop, Tuck, the sheriff, and the Merry Men. The catch was, we hadn't seen or heard from any of them. So, survival required a hell of a lot of improvising.

"Just like the Battle of Montgisard." Lady Winthrop patted my hand as we were shoved down a corridor.

To my dismay, we were quickly separated. Lady Winthrop was ushered down the corridor, while I was pushed toward a huge balcony.

"Smile, darling," the prince snarled. "And don't forget, these three will be watching your every move."

He indicated the huge guards lurking in the shadows, knives at the ready.

With that, he shoved me out onto the balcony and greeted the public.

"Wave, my queen," he grunted through his fake smile.

I kept my hands at my sides and my expression as bleak as it had been all morning. No way was I going to show any support for this snake.

The crowd seemed to have adopted a similar strategy. Instead of meeting the prince with a roar of approval, they offered dark looks and beleaguered grunts.

"Hmm. Your adoring public isn't so adoring. I wonder why that might be?" I muttered.

Prince John tried on a new smile, but the result was more *bared teeth* than *happy to be here.*

"They don't know what's best for them."

I snorted. "Oh, I think they do. And they know poison when they see it."

Hundreds of people packed the town square, gazing up at the balcony where the prince and I stood. It sickened me to think of being paraded out like that in the future.

So, we end this today, my unicorn side vowed. *No matter what it takes.*

But how? I looked down as Bess and her children were pushed into a shallow tub not far below and to my left — the kind used by tanners to treat leather. But instead of a quicklime solution, the tub was filled with an inch of oil that splashed and slurped as Bess was forced in, clutching her two youngest.

Twenty feet above her, on a wide section of the castle wall that served as a second balcony, Lady Thornton stood with a burning torch. All she had to do was drop it, and Bess and her family would be burned alive.

But that was only her second sick insurance policy.

"No! Please!" Bess screamed as one of Lady Thornton's men dragged Tom up an exterior staircase in plain view of everyone. Halfway up to where Lady Thornton stood on the parapet, the guard stopped and held a knife to the boy's throat.

The sheriff stood stiffly at Lady Thornton's side, and she turned to him, fluttering her eyelashes.

The moment anything fishy happens, they die, Lady Thornton's gleeful expression said.

I formed fists with my hands so tightly, my knuckles threatened to rip out of my skin. And as for the sheriff... Never had I seen a dragon rage so close to the surface without actually breaking through. He practically shook with the effort it took not to throttle Lady Thornton. A good thing she had turned away for a word with her guards.

He's a dragon shifter. I have no idea what Robynne sees in him, but they're secretly an item, Tuck had told me. *Anyway, he's on our side,* he'd added begrudgingly.

That made him our ace, but his hands were as tied as mine were — figuratively, at least.

A trumpet blared, and every head turned as Robynne Hood was brought into the square in a creaky wagon.

"Robynne Hood! Robynne Hood!" people cried, murmured, and wailed.

"Pretty clear whose side they're on," I muttered to the prince.

He shrugged. "It doesn't matter what they think, want, or need. She dies today. One way or another."

He pointed to the gallows erected at the far end of the square, then at a group of five archers on a section of wall near it. All had their arrows nocked and aimed at Robynne.

"Insurance," the prince gloated. "In case those Merry Men of hers try anything."

I glanced hopelessly toward Lady Winthrop, who'd been brought out to join the sheriff. The prince and Lady Thornton had thought of everything, it seemed. No matter what we tried, death was inevitable, at least for Robynne and whoever else stood in the way of that evil duo's plans.

"You disgust me," I muttered, but the prince just laughed.

"Oh, I cannot wait for our wedding night."

I clamped my lips in a tight line. If I failed to kill him today, I would do it then. My only regret would be not being able to kill him twice.

"Robynne!" women wailed as their heroine was led to the gallows.

Her step was loose and easy, though her expression was serious.

"Brave, isn't she?" someone in the crowd murmured.

The prince made a face.

"Never thought Robin Hood could be a she," a man in the crowd murmured.

I rolled my eyes. Of course he hadn't.

The bailiff thumped a heavy staff on the wooden platform of the gallows, calling everyone to order.

"Hear ye, hear ye. On this day of our Lord, the twenty-third of February, 1194..."

Everyone strained to listen over the sound of a few late arrivals — a group of cloaked men on horseback. Supporters of Prince John, no doubt, coming to enjoy the spectacle. I shot them a dirty look.

Meanwhile, the bailiff droned on.

"...the right honorable John, Prince of all Britain, Lord of Ireland, and Count of Poitou..."

"Every title but king," I observed dryly.

"Soon," the prince muttered. "Very, very soon."

"...His Excellency the prince has proclaimed the following sentence for the outlaw, Robynne Hood. He — er, she —"

Half the women in the crowd rolled their eyes.

"—she shall be hanged until dead, with her body to remain hanging for three days in warning to those who may mimic her dastardly crimes. Afterward, she shall be drawn and quartered, then cast into a fire. May God have mercy on her soul."

Gasps went out from the public, and many made the sign of the cross in the air.

Robynne didn't so much as frown. She simply looked at Bess and the children, then at the sheriff. I was deaf to whatever mind-talk they exchanged, but it was easy enough to imagine her telling him, *It's not worth it. We can't risk the children.*

I fingered the knife hidden up my sleeve. Maybe if I struck the prince down now, it would catch everyone off guard and foil Lady Thornton's backup plans.

But I could see her fingers clutch the torch attentively, and the guard with a knife to Tom's throat was itching to act too.

Prince John made a grand gesture and called out to the crowd. "People of Nottingham, mark this day. Let the word spread throughout my lands, and let this criminal be a lesson to all my subjects."

Robynne snorted and called back in a strong, steady voice.

"Ah, but these are not your lands, nor your people. They are the king's."

A ripple of approval went through the crowd, though the prince sneered.

"The king? The king does not serve his people. He abandoned them for the Crusades, only to be captured for his folly. How does that serve his people?"

Angry mumbles went through the crowd, but they shushed to hear Robynne's reply.

"Indeed, the king has neglected his people. But let us not examine him in his absence. Let us examine you, Prince. What have *you* done to serve the people? Nothing. On the contrary, you levy oppressive taxes. You allow gangs to terrorize the people in your name while lawlessness spreads."

The prince laughed. "You, a bandit, calling me lawless?"

She nodded firmly. "Yes, because we serve the people in the name of our rightful king, Richard. Yes, we take from the rich — but we give to the poor, or we save for His Majesty's ransom. How much have *you* collected?"

Jeers broke out as Prince John hemmed and hawed.

"My only regret is not to live to see the day our king returns and justice is dealt." With that, Robynne turned to the crowd. "Who is the criminal here, and who is the one who serves you? Not him, I say. Not you, Prince."

An old man pointed at the prince. "Not you. Not you."

A group of young men chimed in, and soon, the chant boomed across the square, punctuated by fingers that stabbed the air.

"Not you! Not you!"

The more voices joined the chant, the more frightening it became. Prince John shrank back.

Every man, woman, and child in the crowd joined in, making the war-horses that had arrived late throw their heads and stamp their feet.

Ha. Let the prince's men feel the wrath of the people. Let them see the future that awaited them.

My heart swelled with hope. If the crowd grew unruly enough, Robynne might have a chance to escape. Bess and her children, too. Maybe even me.

But Lady Thornton, damn her, must have anticipated the same. At a snap of her fingers, one of her archers lit an arrow from her torch, then sent it flying over the heads of the crowd.

With a hard thunk, it buried itself in the frame of the gallows, right beside Robynne, who didn't so much as flinch.

Once again, I dearly wished I'd had a chance to get to know her. Surely she, like Willa, was a woman I could relate to.

The flaming arrow stunned the crowd into silence, giving Lady Thornton's voice a void to fill.

"Pretty words, indeed, from a criminal who makes it appear that you, people of Nottingham, have a say in the matter. You do not. Your only option is to obey your regent or die."

Prince John frowned as if to complain, *I was about to say that.*

I leaned over to hiss to him. "You find her annoying? Just wait until the day she slits your throat."

A guard pushed a knifepoint into my back, but I held my contemptuous gaze steady. Even if I failed in everything else today, I could at least drive apart those two cruel allies.

Lady Thornton nodded to one of her men, who brought the knife closer to young Tom's throat.

Bess screamed. "No! I beg you! No!"

Lady Thornton jerked her chin at the prince, and her eyes blazed with a clear message. *Hurry up and give the signal, you fool. It's time to end this.*

I clamped my hand over the prince's, pinning it to the balcony in the first voluntary contact I'd made. Any delay I created gave the crowd a chance to rebel.

He tried to yank it away, but I held firm. So firm, he stared at me while pulling helplessly at it.

"What is that? Witchcraft?"

I gave him a dry chuckle. "No, just the power of a woman who will do anything to stop you."

A white lie, because much of the power coursing through me at that moment came from the ring that practically burned my finger. The Ring of Aquitaine, a gift from the king himself.

'Tis a family heirloom, and my mother's favorite, he'd said at the time. *May it serve you and this country well.*

I'd been honored beyond words, because the king's mother was Eleanor of Aquitaine, a legend in her own time. Prince

John was her son too, but I couldn't imagine she approved of his leadership style.

"Surprised that a woman can wield such power?" I smirked.

The prince's face went so crimson with anger, I thought he would punch me with his free hand. Unfortunately, he found a better use for it, giving the executioner the signal to proceed.

My blood went cold, because this was the end.

Thank goodness a shrill voice rang out first.

"Wait! Wait!"

The crowd murmured, looking toward the source. A thin, pale monk in a brown robe — one of a dozen men standing below the wall where Lady Thornton, the sheriff, and Lady Winthrop stood.

"And who are you?" Prince John demanded.

The man threw his hood back and gave a little bow. "Friar Cyril, at your service. Before you proceed, we must pray for this poor, wayward soul."

I stared. Cyril, the monk with the naughty artwork?

His group was made up of ten equally pale, scrawny monks plus two big, hulking ones. My mouth cracked open, and my heart leaped.

Tuck? And John the bear shifter? With those deep, heavy hoods hiding their faces, there was no way to be sure.

"And who is *we*?" Prince John called impatiently.

Cyril grinned and motioned to his companions. "Just me and a select few of my fellow clergy. And in all humility, sir, I can assure you we are Winslow Abbey's finest choir."

Chapter Twenty

TUCK

I whispered to John, correcting Cyril's words. "Winslow Abbey's *only* choir."

"Shh!" the big bear shifter hissed.

The scars on his hand turned white as he gripped the quarterstaff hidden in his robes.

I couldn't risk raising my head to find Marian on the balcony, but I did lift my eyes. And there she stood, just visible beyond the edge of my hood.

My mate, my lion sighed.

She looked just as fierce and defiant as she had that first night, when I'd surprised her in the library.

My heart thumped. Was that truly only a short time ago? Well, that had been enough. Just those first few moments in her presence had changed my life forever. And after everything we'd experienced together...

My inner lion swished his tail, and my body warmed. My beast growled at the sight of her gripping the prince's hand, but I knew she had no choice. Judging by the way her right sleeve bulged, she had a knife ready to go, too.

In spite of everything, I grinned and threw a message into her mind.

I know you haven't been waiting around for some random man to rescue you, and I'm sure you have a brilliant plan worked out, but my friends and I would love to join the party if you don't mind. No strings attached.

Her relief was audible.

Plan? I wish. I'm improvising. As for lending a hand, yes please! Also, I'm starting to change my mind about strings — as long as they attach to you.

I burned to see the prince get his comeuppance — but the question was, how would we outsmart the multiple backups he and Lady Thornton had in place? We needed something to throw them off guard — somehow. Even something tiny.

Too risky, I told Marian, sensing her prepare to draw her knife.

Every option is risky, she shot back.

True. Especially now that the first part of our plan had failed. Alan was supposed to fly in and set off an attack. But he was nowhere in sight.

Despite the chill of that winter day, I broke out in a sweat. The choir was getting to the end of their hymn, and still, no Alan in sight. John was moving his lips to the tune, but even he looked ready to explode.

Where the hell is he? the bear shifter fretted.

I scanned the sky. Our whole plan hinged on Alan creating a diversion — right now.

The minute the singing stops, I'll charge and free Bess, John muttered.

I shook my head. *Even you can't beat a dropped torch. And that guard will slit Tom's throat.*

Marian and the prince stood on a balcony a good thirty feet from us. Not quite as far up, the sheriff, Lady Thornton, and Lady Winthrop occupied a wider part of the parapet that connected to ground level by stairs, where young Tom was being held.

We hadn't been able to communicate our plans to Robynne or the sheriff, but I could tell he was barely holding back. Something had to give, and soon.

"A-men." The choir hit their final note and held it.

...and held it, and held it, because that was Alan's cue.

But Alan was nowhere in sight.

I shifted my weight from foot to foot, ready to morph into lion form.

"...nnnnnn," Cyril dragged out the last note, turning red. One by one, the singers broke off and gasped for air. Cyril gallantly sang on, but even he started to peter out.

Still no Alan. My fingers twitched, eager to turn into claws.

When the hymn faded for good, Lady Thornton signaled the prince to move things along. He opened his mouth to shout an order, and—

On the parapet, Lady Winthrop brought a hand to her brow and fluttered her eyes. "Oh goodness. I'm beginning to feel faint."

One moment, she was wobbling in place. The next, she was toppling down the stairs.

"Lady Winthrop!" Marian screamed, genuinely afraid.

I gaped. Lady Winthrop made it look good, but that was definitely an expert fall, because fainting didn't make you cartwheel all the way down the stairs. As kids, my brothers and I had staged all kinds of dramatic fights, and we'd milked the falling down the stairs gag for all it was worth.

My poor mother. She'd fallen for it every time.

A little like the crowd in the square now — and most importantly, the soldier holding a knife to young Tom's throat. Lady Winthrop careened past Tom and right into the soldier, knocking him clear off the stairs.

"Go! Go!" I shoved John.

"Oh dear." Lady Winthrop picked herself up off the groaning soldier. "You aren't hurt, are you?"

Ha. I'd seen her elbow him in the groin after he'd cushioned her fall.

Not that I had time to admire her work. Our plan had just been launched, and I had work to do.

Soldiers rushed forward, but John and I bounded up the stairs, knocking them out of the way. The moment we were hidden behind the front face of the parapet, we dropped to all fours and shifted.

Usually, the process took a few painful seconds, with skin giving way to fur, bones finding a new configuration, and teeth extending into fangs. And usually, I would pause to give my mane a good shake. But there was no time for any of that now. In the space of one breath, I went from running upright to sprinting on all fours, trailed by a long, tufted tail.

While I raced left toward Lady Thornton, John, in bear form, rushed along the wall in the opposite direction, heading for the archers. The first two turned their bows on him, but their shots went wide. A heartbeat later, cries erupted as John mowed them down.

So, whew. That eliminated one layer of Prince John's backup plans.

I ran on, cursing every inch that separated me from Marian on that too-distant, too-high balcony. I cursed the guards too — the ones who jumped out of the shadows and grabbed her when she pulled a knife on Prince John.

"Marian!" I roared — literally.

But the prince yelled at the same time. "Archers! Prepare!"

Three men appeared atop the castle's tallest tower and aimed at Robynne. Yet another backup plan?

Willa! John bellowed.

His mate had leaped to the gallows and shoved the executioner aside. Then she produced a knife and started sawing at Robynne's bonds.

All according to plan, except the archers were supposed to be eliminated by then. Now, both women were totally exposed to the archers atop the tower.

"No!" someone in the crowd cried, spotting the new danger.

Other bystanders pointed to the archers, while a handful tackled the executioner before he could return to his post.

"Shoot! Kill them both!" the prince yelled, indicating Robynne and Willa.

John started sprinting in their direction, but there was no way a bear could outrace an arrow.

A dragon, however...

The sheriff jumped to the edge of the parapet and raised his arms. The crowd broke out in confused murmurs, then screams when his arms stretched and transformed to wings. His face stretched too, extending until human features gave way to the muzzle of a dragon.

A very angry, very dangerous dragon who took to the air with powerful wingbeats.

I wasn't sure whether to cheer or despair. Revealing our shifter sides was a last-ditch measure. But things could hardly get more *last-ditch* than now.

The crowd screamed and ducked. A few ran, but most were transfixed by the sight of a mighty dragon swooping over their heads. Hats flew, cloaks whipped, and hair was blasted by every powerful wingbeat.

Of course, *swoop* wasn't the best word for the short distance the dragon covered — more of a *hop* for a creature that big and powerful — but it might as well have been *soaring* to the humans witnessing it. Those closest to the gallows screamed and ran for cover as the dragon approached, creating an open space in the crowded square. He landed there, held his wings wide in a protective shield for Robynne and Willa, then whirled to face the archers.

I dare you to shoot, his roar said, backed up by long plumes of fire. *I dare you to make me even more angry.*

I was too busy rushing toward Marian to look up, but an arrow plonked off the stonework near my side. It hadn't been shot, just dropped. So, yes — the archers were terrified.

An eagle dive-bombed them for good measure — Alan, finally arriving to help.

All good news, but two targets remained exposed: Marian and Bess's family. The latter was still huddled below Lady Thornton and that blazing torch.

I sprinted, only steps from that madwoman now. She whirled and held the torch over Bess's whimpering family.

"Stop, or they'll burn alive!" she screamed.

I didn't stop. I couldn't. Each of us had his or her assigned task, and mine was to free Marian. I had to focus on that and trust others to accomplish their jobs.

But, yikes. That scared me to death, because Bess's fate rested in the hands of our weakest link.

I roared, launching myself at Lady Thornton. Her eyes went wide in shock, and her voice turned to a vengeful howl.

"If I die, they die," she screamed, dropping the torch.

I flinched as it disappeared over the wall, mentally preparing myself for agonized screams to erupt. But none came. Even Lady Thornton did a double take, peering over the wall.

Bess crouched, hands over her head, children clutched close. The torch fell, leaving a red streak in the air. I braced myself for the *whoosh* and burst of heat that would follow the torch hitting the oil.

But at the last possible moment, a man stuck out a hand, caught the torch, and thrust it safely to one side.

"No!" Lady Thornton screamed.

Robert looked up with an insolent grin. "Yes." Then he jumped to Bess's side. "Let's get you out of here, shall we?"

Ah, good old Robert, charming as ever.

All that happened in the space of two heartbeats while I leaped at Lady Thornton. Then, *bang!* I crashed into her with my teeth bared.

Finish her, my lion growled, going for the jugular.

But something sliced into my ribs, and my roar ended on a choke. I stared at the blood seeping from my belly and cursed.

Ah, Lady Thornton, conniving as ever. Now I knew why she hadn't shifted to wolf form. She needed her hands for that knife.

Well, fine. I had already accepted death as inevitable, right? As long as Marian survived.

Except, oh. Maybe I'd lucked out, because that wound wasn't as deep as I'd feared. So, huh. A lucky break — at last.

I bared my teeth for a second attack. One I vowed wouldn't miss. I leaped at Lady Thornton, reaching with claws and fangs. As she stumbled backward, the air shimmered, signaling her impending shift. But she arched abruptly and screamed — a move so awkward and out of place, I was sure it was a trick.

"Lady Thornton," the guard behind her gasped.

She fell, impaled by the weapon of one of her own men. A fitting end, I thought.

Her eyes crossed on the sword tip protruding from her chest, while her hands clutched at the rest, buried hilt-deep in her back.

"You fool," she hissed, clawing at the stonework and gasping for air.

I winced at my wound, then backed up for a running jump at the balcony where Marian and the prince stood. As satisfying as it would be to watch Lady Thornton die, I had no time. Not with my mate's life on the line.

For a moment, I flew gracefully through the air. Then, *bang!* I slammed into the side of the balcony, barely hanging on to the upper edge with my claws. With a grunt, I hauled myself up and over, then tumbled to the inside.

"Tuck!" Marian cried, not so much *Happy to see you* as *Watch out*, so I did.

The nearest guard came at me, but Marian kicked him aside. Another guard was dragging himself indoors, bleeding from a knife wound.

Good old Marian. As fierce and capable as ever.

She was grappling with a third guard and rapidly gaining the upper hand. Otherwise, the balcony was empty. I whirled, bewildered. Where was the prince?

"Inside! He's escaping!" Marian yelled, still busy with the guard.

I leaped over the wounded guard and landed, squinting, on a thick rug. Outside, it had been broad daylight. Inside, it was dim enough that my eyes needed a moment to adjust.

A moment that nearly killed me, because a battle-axe came whamming down out of nowhere. I rolled just in time for it to slice the rug in two instead of me. When a head went rolling, I did a double take, then snarled. That rug wasn't a rug. It was a tiger pelt, still attached to the head — until now. As a lion, I wasn't especially fond of tigers, but still. No feline deserved such an indignity.

Doubly furious, I scrambled to my paws, cutting off the prince from the doorway. For a moment, he yanked at the axe, buried deep in the floor. Giving up, he snatched a sword from the wall display and raised it as I came flying at him.

Bang! I tackled him. Momentum carried us out to the balcony, where the prince was thrust back against the ornamental balustrade. The sword fell behind him, where the crowd scattered. I crashed into his chest, all but snickering. Now, I had the bastard.

When the air shimmered around his shoulders, I growled louder. *I dare you to shift. I dare you.*

Suffice to say, he didn't.

I opened my jaws wide, ready to tear out his throat, when a voice boomed out like a cannon.

"Stop!"

It was so deep, so thoroughly commanding, I froze.

Beside me, Marian did the same. One foot, she kept on the stone floor of the balcony. The other pinned down the guard she'd just subdued. She stared at me, then down into the square.

Moments ago, the place had been sheer pandemonium. Now, everyone hushed — the humans fleeing for the exits, and even Daniel, the dragon, who turned to face the new danger.

Hundreds of eyes turned with him. Even Prince John rolled his eyes awkwardly up and to the side to peer down from his arched-back position.

I growled, ignoring the distraction. No one and nothing would keep me from killing Prince John now that I had the chance.

But just as I was about to tear out his throat, that voice boomed out a second time.

"Stop! In the name of the king!"

My teeth clacked together in the air as I yanked myself back, staring. What was that again?

At the back of the square, the mounted men — those late arrivals — pushed forward. Their steeds snorted in warning, and the crowd parted before them.

Everyone focused on the man at the head of that phalanx. Even from this distance, I could sense his confidence and power.

A travel cloak covered him from head to toe — one so big, it even concealed much of his steed. As he rode slowly forward, he signaled to a page, who stopped, holding a corner of the cloak. It slipped free as the rider advanced, revealing a magnificent white horse and the rider's true identity.

Hundreds of onlookers gasped, then fell to one knee.

"King Richard!"

"King Richard!"

The name echoed across the square, carried from one startled onlooker to another.

I was as stunned as anyone — except the widest-eyed of us
all: Prince John.

He stared, then peeped in disbelief. "Richard?"

Marian half cheered, half slumped in relief. "Richard!"

Chapter Twenty-One

TUCK

For a moment, the sound of that hallowed name rang out over the square. Then the great man jutted his pointy, silver-streaked beard, making everyone fall silent. His horse's harness and armor jangled as it strode toward the balcony.

Marian elbowed me. "It's the king. You have to bow."

I shook my head. Not if it meant releasing the prince, who would surely pull some kind of trick.

King Richard peered around in disapproval. His dark eyes were framed by eyebrows that rose and fell in little Vs, intensifying that look that said, *I am not amused.*

The men behind him threw off their cloaks, revealing armor, shields, and flags emblazoned with three golden lions — the royal insignia.

The king turned slowly, taking in every detail, from Bess's huddled family to the dragon standing defiantly by the gallows and the two bold women beside it — Robynne and Willa. Then he swept his gaze over the bear on the parapet, the trembling archers on the tower, and finally, to the balcony. There, his eyes narrowed on the spectacle of me, in lion form, pinning the prince to the balustrade.

My stomach sank. One didn't exactly tell a king, *I swear, I can explain!* Because, yikes. That was his brother I was about to kill.

His king only brightened — and only momentarily — when he spotted the woman I loved.

"Marian!"

She gave a cheery wave. "Richard!"

I stared. She was on a first-name basis with the king? I doubted his wife called him anything but *Your Majesty.* Then again, they didn't spend much time together.

And just like that, I felt sorry for him. Yes, him, the king. He might be a Crusader knight and king of England, duke of Aquitaine, Poitiers, Normandy, and who knew what else, but he didn't have his true love.

Then I gulped, because neither did I. The moment the dust settled over the mess of this day, it would be over. I would head back to the abbey, and Marian would return to her manor house, both of us with only memories for company.

Suddenly, spending the rest of my life celibate didn't seem like a problem. If I couldn't have Marian, I didn't want anyone.

Marian waved to one of the men accompanying the king. "Father!"

Both men waved while hundreds of people looked on, including me. I'd grown up in a noble family, but wow. Hers really did hobnob with royalty.

When the king's gaze returned to his brother, he sighed. "John."

Robynne always sighed her younger brother's name, but always with a solid dose of exasperated, yet heartfelt love. Richard's sigh for his brother...not so much.

"Thank the Lord you're back!" John squeaked. "This beast was about to kill me."

The king's eyes turned to me and stayed there a while. "Indeed."

I snorted, holding my ground. The prince deserved to die, and he knew it.

"Well, aren't you going to stop him?" the prince demanded of his brother.

The king considered. And considered...

Every man, woman, and child in the square held their breath for his verdict, though none more feverishly than I.

"Perhaps," the king murmured. "Perhaps not."

"Richard!" the prince squeaked.

The king tilted his head, studying his brother. "What on earth are you doing?"

He didn't end the question with *idiot*, but his tone did.

"I'm keeping law and order."

"Clearly," Richard muttered dryly. Then he snapped his fingers and boomed, "You have three minutes to get down here. All of you." Then he looked at me, and his frown deepened. "And make sure you come properly attired."

I gulped and murmured an inner, *Yes, sir.*

The prince, still half hanging over the balustrade, poked me in the ribs. "You heard him. Release me."

I growled, but Marian raised the sword she'd snatched from one of the guards. "Don't worry. I'll keep an eye on him."

Reluctantly, I backed away from the prince, who straightened his clothes and whisked away the slobber I'd left on his cloak.

Heathen, his entitled expression sniffed.

I growled, hurrying him along.

I remained in lion form all the way to the main door, where I shifted and pulled on the robe Cyril tossed to me — the one I'd discarded earlier.

"I can't believe it. You're a lion?" Cyril gaped.

Lion. Dreamer. Knight. Shifter. All those parts of me I'd had to lock away for so long. Parts I would have to lock away again soon — forever.

Lover, my lion mourned, watching Marian.

She skipped forward eagerly, while the prince and I dragged our heels before bowing stiffly before the king.

"Richard!" Marian repeated joyously as he leaned down from his saddle for a hug. Then she ran to her father, who dismounted and threw his arms wide for an embrace.

They hugged a long time, swaying from side to side.

Despite the sorrow and despair choking my soul, I smiled. What a beautiful thing love was.

Her father cleared his throat and pulled back to touch her cheek.

"Good to see you, my dear."

Lord Winthrop was there too, waving casually to his wife. "Oh hello, darling. Everything all right?"

She brushed the dust off her sleeve. "Of course. And you?"

"Fine, fine."

One might have thought she'd spilled some tea when he'd bumped into a chair rather than risking their lives for king and country.

"Thank goodness you're back," Prince John gushed, bowing so low, his nose nearly hit the ground.

I growled under my breath.

"Indeed," the king muttered, unimpressed. "And not a moment too soon, it seems."

By then, the prince was dripping sweat. "Yes. I've captured the outlaw, Robynne Hood, as you can see."

"Oh, I have seen plenty," the king growled. "I have heard too. All that I need to know." He raised a hand, hushing the prince, and motioned two soldiers forward. "Lock him up."

"But, Richard..." the prince pleaded.

"Enough!" the king roared, making Prince John wince. "I will deal with you later. Perhaps I'll be feeling more charitable then."

The prince opened his mouth, but the king silenced him with a few words.

"Or feeling less charitable. Your gamble."

The prince sagged, and I growled under my breath as the soldiers led him away.

Next time we meet, I promised, *you will die.*

A soft clap sounded as he was dragged toward the dungeon. Then another and another, much like the patter of rain. As more and more people joined in, the applause became a deluge, making it clear how the people felt about Prince John.

At one firm look from the king, however, the applause died.

"And who is this?" He glared at me.

Marian pulled me to my feet and patted my chest. "This is Tuck."

I loved how she sang my name and held me close, but clearly, the king didn't approve.

"*Friar* Tuck," she added, as if that would help.

The king laughed. "Friar? This man is no more a friar than I am the trumpeter's mother." Then he turned to a man near the rear of his train. "No offense, Basil."

"None taken, sir." The man saluted, making the flag on his trumpet wave.

The king went back to glaring at me. Nothing I took personally since he seemed to glare at everyone except Marian. Still, my knees wobbled, and my inner lion quietly tucked in its tail.

He hmpfed, then steered his horse toward Bess. "Are you all right, madam?"

Bess barely glanced his way. She was too busy gazing into Robert's eyes. Apparently, the feeling was mutual, because Robert stared back, equally tongue-tied.

"He saved me," Bess breathed.

Robert smiled. She smiled. Their hands were clasped, their cheeks flushed. Clearly, those two were in their own world, even with the children gathered around them.

"Indeed," the king murmured, hiding a smile that suggested he was finally amused.

Marian towed me along as she introduced the others.

"This is my friend Willa, and her partner, John Little..."

Both bowed deeply.

The king nodded, gliding past on his horse.

"You remember Lady Thornton," Marian murmured darkly at the body slumped on the stairs.

The king didn't give her a second glance. "I try to forget."

"And this, I believe, is Nottingham's sheriff, and Robynne Hood." Marian grinned at them both, then whispered to Robynne, "Good to finally meet you."

Robynne smiled back. "Good to meet *you*." Then she hastened into a curtsy.

Daniel, now in human form and robed, bowed deeply to the king. "Daniel Cook, sir. Acting sheriff."

The king snorted. "If that was acting, I fear to witness the real thing."

Your average man might preen and strut, but Daniel barely nodded. A class act in every way.

When Robynne reached into her boot and produced a knife, three of the king's men leaped forward, and the crowd gasped. But the king threw up a hand, letting Robynne speak.

"Sire." She kept her head down while holding the knife up. "It's good to have you back."

I grinned, as did the king. I'd heard the story of that knife from one of the Merry Men. Apparently, the king had passed through Locksley when Robynne was a little girl, and she'd so impressed him that he'd given her his own knife — one with a lion etched onto the hilt.

"Ah, yes. The young warrior. I remember you," the king chuckled, definitely amused — and impressed.

Robynne looked up with a smile. "I remember you too."

His laugh echoed over the hushed crowd.

"That was quite a speech for an outlaw. Bold words," he observed.

Her throat bobbed. "All from the heart, sir. We never gave up on you. We never will."

A lump formed in my throat, because Robynne was speaking for all of us.

None of us gave up on you, I wanted to echo. *Robynne, most of all.*

I thought of all the sacrifices she and Daniel had made for so long, praying they would finally get their happy ending. They deserved it more than anyone.

"I don't doubt it," the king replied, gifting Robynne with a tiny bow of his own.

She grinned and reached for Daniel's hand.

Everyone waited. What would the king say, do, command?

He looked around, as if noticing the crowd for the first time.

"I don't know what I expected to find in Nottingham, but I certainly didn't expect this."

Polite chuckles came from the crowd until he straightened, ready to make a pronouncement.

"I suppose all that remains is to decide what to do about all this." He looked around, scowling, then added, "And with my brother."

Everyone glanced at the gallows in a hint the king either missed or ignored.

Ignored, I decided. The man didn't miss anything. Like Marian's hand, still firmly around mine. His eyebrow quirked at that, but then he turned back to the crowd.

"People of Nottingham..."

Everyone waited, barely moving.

"Let it be known that I absolve the outlaw, Robynne Hood, of any charges brought against her."

Applause broke out, though the king extinguished it with a quick motion.

"Further, I believe your acting sheriff may be the right man for the job. What say you?"

An electrified buzz went through the crowd, which regarded Daniel with a mixture of respect and fear.

"Well, what say you?" the king demanded.

Tense silence settled over the square, and Marian and I exchanged worried glances. What now?

Chapter Twenty-Two

TUCK

The king pointed impatiently at a man at the front of the crowd. "You there. What do you have to say?"

The man yanked off his cap and twisted it in his hands. "He's done a fine job, sir. Much better than the last sheriff."

I snorted. That wouldn't be difficult.

Countless onlookers nodded, though their support was muted.

Dispersed whispers emerged from the crowd. "Fair... Tolerant... Strict but understanding..."

"But...?" The king circled his hand impatiently.

The man continued twisting his cap. "Well, you've seen it yourself, sir. He's a dragon."

"And that big one over there is a bear." Someone else indicated John.

A third pointed to me. "Him, too. I saw him turn into a lion."

I stood perfectly still, because what exactly did one say to something like that? *Yes, as a matter of fact. I am a lion. Want to hear me roar?*

I sighed inwardly. Probably not a good time.

"They're wild animals, sir. It's just not natural."

My heart sank, and I fully expected the king to nod solemnly.

But he didn't. Instead, he grinned — grinned! — then winked.

"My dear man, why do you suppose they call me Lion-heart?"

I stared. Robynne stared. Daniel too. Everyone stared — except Marian, the king's men, and a woman at the side of the crowd, who fainted. So technically, she wasn't staring. But the other however-many-hundred people did.

"You mean... you mean..." A handful of people backed away, but most held their ground.

The king sighed loudly enough for everyone to hear. "Consider the evidence. Who did these animals, as you call them, fight for? *What* did they fight for?"

Nervous murmurs sounded, though no one spoke up. No one but Robynne.

"We fight for the people of Nottingham. For our king. For justice. We always have, and we always will."

More staring ensued, and someone whispered, "We?"

Robynne touched her chest. "Fox shifter."

For a moment, everyone remained speechless. Then Marge, the stout, bossy basket vendor, spoke in a voice honed from years of calling out over the din of the marketplace, "Ha. A fox and a woman. No wonder she's so cunning."

Her tone applauded Robynne, who grinned back.

"But..." a man murmured.

Marge elbowed him. "But nothing. Without Robynne Hood, we wouldn't have fed the children this winter. And without the sheriff extending the deadline, we would still be scraping pennies together for taxes instead of milk and bread."

The king shot a stern look at Daniel, who gulped. "Short-term extension, sir. Enough to get your subjects through the winter."

I sucked in a breath at the subtext: *The subjects you haven't been here to look after.*

To his credit, the king looked penitent. Hopefully, the message that he was needed at home more than at the Crusades was coming through loud and clear.

"But... but... They can't be trusted," someone else said.

"Trust?" a rotund, strangely pale man retorted, drawing everyone's attention.

It took a moment, but I finally placed him — the baker from Nottingham's east gate, father of the local beauty, Mary. And, wow. Who knew bakers could be such passionate orators?

"For years, our lives have been in the hands of thieves who have done nothing but tax and torment us," he said. "They speak pretty words, but their actions tell a different tale. Things have only improved since the sheriff stepped in, together with the good Lady Robynne. So, trust? I know who I trust. Don't you?"

"But she's a bandit," someone muttered.

"A bandit who's kept food coming in for my children, no thanks to the likes of you," another woman retorted. Then her eyes slid to the king.

The king nodded at the unspoken accusation. "Even a king cannot be everywhere and serve everyone, no matter how he desires. Thus, I am grateful for those who have worked in my name — those of true heart and loyal soul." He nodded firmly at Daniel and Robynne. Then he took a deep breath and went on. "Good people of Nottingham, judge for yourselves. Who do you prefer at your side — these shifters or your previous overlords?"

A ripple of affirmation went through the crowd, and Marge crossed her arms.

"I'll take Robynne any day. And that sheriff, too." She blew him a kiss. "Much fairer than our last one, and much easier on the eyes. Don't you agree, ladies?"

Giggles broke out, and while the men looked annoyed, their respect for Daniel was clear.

"There it is, then," the king proclaimed. "Mr. Cook here is duly appointed Nottingham's official sheriff, and Miss Hood, your newest alderman." Then he scratched his head. "Or is it alderwoman?"

Robynne bowed. "Alderwoman works for me — but only if the people of Nottingham agree."

"Three cheers for Robynne Hood!" someone cried.

Everyone chimed in enthusiastically. "Hip hip hooray! Hip hip hooray! Hip hip hooray!"

Her cheeks went red, and she drew a line in the dirt with her foot. Humility was just one reason she would be perfect for the job as a town councillor.

So, whew. I looked around. There it was — the happy ending we'd barely dared to hope for. Marian was safe. Robynne was acquitted. Bess and the children had been saved. Prince John was imprisoned, and the king had promoted Daniel from *acting* to *official* sheriff of Nottingham.

It was everything I'd hoped for, and more. A happy ending for everyone. . . except me.

I swallowed hard, not daring to look at Marian. The wound on my belly was already healing, so my only regret was not dying honorably, because now I had to find a way to live without Marian.

My lion growled so loudly, the sound slipped out, and the nearest dozen people jumped away.

"Um. . . sorry," I said a little sheepishly.

Marian squeezed my hand, but I didn't have it in me to squeeze back. I didn't even have it in me to look up. Hundreds of innocent townsfolk had just seen shapeshifters for the first time in their lives, and they'd witnessed the return of the king. I didn't need to add a crying lion to the spectacle.

"Well, I believe that's everything," the king concluded.

His horse perked its ears and shuffled, ready to carry the great man to his next pressing engagement. A battle, perhaps, or a coronation. . .

My lion sighed.

"Not quite everything," said the only person brave enough to contradict the king — Marian.

He looked perplexed. "No? What, then?"

"There was a wedding planned for tomorrow. . ." she said.

The king snorted. "Surely you have no interest in my weasel of a brother."

She shook her head and pulled my hand to her heart, cupping it with both her hands. "Not in the least. But I did have my eye on a fair knight."

My heart thumped, hoping against hope.

The king frowned. "You mean this rascal?"

She nodded. "Tuck."

The king glared at me. "Your real name."

My old self was so deeply buried in my subconscience, it took me a few seconds to reply. "Friar Tuck, sir. Formerly Mark Tuckerton."

The king did a double take. "Henry and Alice's boy?"

I stared. That he recognized my family name wasn't terribly surprising. But that he knew my parents?

Wow. Next time I saw them, I would have a *lot* of questions.

"Interesting," he murmured. "Very interesting."

I hung my head. It wasn't interesting. It was tragic, because I loved Marian, but I couldn't have her.

Then he shook his head. "It pains me to see how poorly my lands have been governed. Robbers became lawmakers, and heroes were forced to become outlaws. Even knights and priests have switched places."

Nervous laughter rippled through the crowd.

"Well, it's time to set things straight. I hereby dismiss you, Friar Tuck, of your ecclesiastical duties — unless, of course, you desire to remain in the priesthood?"

God, no, I nearly shouted. "No. No such desire," I managed.

A few guffaws broke out, terrifying me. I hadn't meant it as a joke, but if the king thought I didn't take his offer seriously...

But, whew. He grinned too.

"No, I didn't think so. However, let me be clear about one thing. I will never allow my goddaughter to marry beneath her station. What say you, William?"

Marian's father shook his head. "Never."

"But, Father!" Marian protested, but the king raised his hand.

"A landless lord is out of the question."

Marian turned red. "I don't care about land, titles, or money."

"Perhaps not, but you are neither king nor queen here," the king said gently.

Marian's father tapped his lips, thinking. "No, that just wouldn't do. But a landed lord..."

I despaired, because my eldest brother stood to inherit everything. I was in line to inherit exactly nothing. Not a single building, nor a title...not even a cow pasture.

"If you please, sir," someone called, making everyone turn — even the king.

"Yes, Sheriff?" he asked Daniel.

"Nottingham hasn't had a lord for quite some time, sir."

I stared at him, then the castle, my mind ticking over slowly. Too slowly, because the connections it made seemed too good to be true. Again and again, I halted the process and went back to the beginning to piece his hints together.

Nottingham. Castle. A vacant lordship...

Whoa. Wait. Was Daniel actually helping me?

He shrugged and spoke into my mind. *Not sure why, but yes. We could use a reasonable lord around here. Assuming you don't abandon us to ride off to the Crusades.*

I shook my head vehemently. *A wise knight taught me about just causes. So, no. My place is here.*

My father had once clapped me on the shoulder and said something along the lines of, *You'll know the day you become a man, my boy. You'll recognize it when the moment arrives.*

For years, I'd been wondering if I had missed that moment or if it had simply passed me by. But now, the realization was clear as a bell.

That day had finally come, and I knew it.

Funny how parents could be right about so many things.

"Well, why didn't you say so?" The king huffed — at me, as if that were my fault.

My lips moved, but I couldn't produce a coherent word.

He flapped a hand. "Rhetorical question. No need to answer." He squinted at me, then at Marian. "He isn't a fool, is he?"

She broke out in a huge smile. "No, sir. Not usually."

"Hmpf." The king considered for another minute, then looked at me skeptically. "Do you think yourself up to such a task?"

I gulped, looking over the crowd, then the castle. Lord of Nottingham?

"Er…well…"

"He's amazing," Marian assured him. "He thinks of everything."

I shook my head. "I usually overlook a critical detail or two. Or three or four… So, no. Whenever I plan, I assume everything will go wrong."

The king laughed. "Spoken like a true crusader."

I blinked. Really?

Marian's father smiled broadly. "I believe he might do — especially if he has the right woman to guide him."

Of course I did. The king could name me lord of the universe, but Marian would always be the boss — and brains — of the operation.

"Oh, he'll have that, believe me." Marian grinned.

Her father gave the king a firm nod. "No man will ever be good enough for my daughter, but I raised her to have a mind of her own, and I will respect that. And, as they say, there's no stopping true love."

Lord and Lady Winthrop grinned at each other and clasped hands. Bess and Robert hugged. Robynne and Daniel bumped shoulders, while John slid an arm around Willa.

The king frowned.

"Come now, Richard," Marian's father coaxed. "What say you?"

I braced myself for something like, *Bah, humbug. Send him back to the abbey, and lock Marian in a convent as far from there as possible.*

Marian's grip on my hand got even tighter, and I nearly yelped.

She didn't say a word, but her eyes begged the king. *Sir…Please…*

The king held out for another long minute, then heaved a weary sigh. "Fine." Then he glared at me. "But if you ever do anything that makes this woman less than splendidly happy, I will have you hung, drawn, quartered—"

Lady Winthrop cleared her throat, cutting him off.

Et cetera, et cetera, his eyes blazed.

I gulped. "I get the picture, sir."

The king nodded grimly. Then he clapped, calling everyone to attention. "I hereby name these two as Lord and Lady of Nottingham, effective tomorrow." Then he looked at me expectantly. "Well?"

I froze, not sure what he meant.

"Kiss the bride, you fool."

Oh. Gladly.

Still, I was so dumb struck, I was slow to move. A damn good thing Marian reeled me in and kissed me. Deeply. Passionately. Heartily.

The crowd broke into applause, cheers, and wolf whistles, but I didn't care. Not with my soul exploding with joy.

"We really get to be together?" I whispered between kisses.

Marian chuckled. "Miracles do happen."

I tuned out everything but her after that, though I didn't miss the crowd's reaction to the king's final announcement.

"Good people of Nottingham, I believe a feast is in order. What say you?"

The crowd broke into jubilant cheers. Out of the corner of my eye, I saw Robynne throw her arms around Daniel. Not far from them, Willa and John kissed. The Merry Men had never looked prouder, and Cyril and the guys from the abbey beamed. I spotted Robert and Bess next, still staring at each other as if that joyous explosion was for them.

And maybe it was. Well, for all of us — everyone, including every citizen of Nottingham. The day we'd dreamed of had finally arrived.

Chapter Twenty-Three

MARIAN

"Oh, Tuck..." I panted as he moved over me.

Morning light streamed in the window, highlighting his bare back...rear...legs... Okay, bare everything. I was just as naked but far less composed, because the things he did to me...

"Yes..." I cried out when he plunged deeper.

Tuck groaned just as loudly, and I nearly shushed him. Then I remembered there was no need. We were in bed — our new, very own bed, in a private chamber high up in the castle — and those walls were thick. So, we could make all the noise we wanted — or needed.

Yes, need, because after all the danger, doubts, and uncertainties of the past days, we needed this moment to bond. Permanently. The unicorn bond had been the first step. But Tuck had promised me a mating bite, and I needed it badly.

"Yes..." I jammed my hips against his.

Every nerve in my body trembled with pleasure and desire. Pleasure from the way he moved inside me, and an overwhelming, greedy desire for more, more, more.

"Tuck..." I cried, arching against him.

He bent, kissing my neck between breathless thrusts. Seeking...

Close... So close. I sensed his lion guiding him.

Blood whooshed through my veins so forcefully, each rushing beat registered in my ears. The pulse in my neck hammered against my skin, calling to him. *Right here...*

Tuck paused, making eye contact. I nodded — a more ladylike option than clawing his back and screaming, *Yes! Now! Please!*

Tuck moved so fast, I didn't even see him dip. One moment, he was looking at me, and the next—

Fangs gouged my skin. The flash of pain was so brief, it only primed me for the rush of pleasure that followed. A hot rush, like a kicked-over bonfire that sent embers tumbling through my veins.

I clamped one hand over his rear, pinning his hips to mine, and the other around his head, desperate to keep him close.

Possessive lion growls sounded in my head, accompanied by images from Tuck's mind. I saw a beautiful woman beside herself in wanton pleasure. A goddess, practically, whose love made him swell with pride and satisfaction.

Which meant that couldn't possibly be me. Except it was. *I* was, at least in Tuck's eyes.

"You are a goddess," he whispered breathlessly.

I was too busy murmuring choppy, incoherent syllables to correct him. Maybe later. If I remembered...

For now, I made sure Tuck glimpsed himself the way I saw him: a muscled, battle-scarred knight, erasing all the heartbreak and loneliness his fair maiden had ever experienced. Erasing it for good, because he was making me his forever.

"Yes..." I whispered.

His feline essence mixed with my equine genes, bonding us for all eternity.

I cried out as he thrust one more time, anchoring himself deep. When he exploded inside me, I clamped on to him, then shuddered with my own release.

All I felt was heat. All I heard were our pounding hearts and heavy breaths. All I sensed was deep, never-ending satisfaction.

"Tuck..." I whispered.

He retracted his fangs, giving me one last aftershock of pleasure. Then he went limp, pressing me into the mattress.

"Marian..." he rasped.

Evidently, there was one thing that could subdue my brave lion: love, radiating with the intensity of the sun on a bright summer day.

Of course, it was only dawn on a midwinter's morning. But not at that moment. Not for me.

We held each other for an eternity. Even after we separated, we gazed into each other's eyes for an equally long time.

Bells clanged in the distance, and Tuck tensed, then started laughing. Harder and harder, until he was rolling in mirth.

"What?" I asked, chuckling just from watching him.

It took him several tries to get the words out. "I thought that was the call to prayer."

I laughed, shaking my head. "Nope. Something much better."

He grinned, pulling me nice and snug against his chest. "Yes. Wedding bells."

I nodded, kissing him. "*Our* wedding bells."

We passed another minute in a happy daze. Then Tuck's hands started wandering over my body again.

"But seeing as those are just pre-wedding bells, I think we have time for some more fun."

I arched an eyebrow. "Are you saying the wedding won't be fun?"

He grinned one of those sunburst smiles. "No, but there's fun, and there's *fun*. The kind of fun that doesn't involve the king, your father, and hundreds of other witnesses."

"Ugh." I pushed the images away. "What a way to kill the mood."

He slid his hands down my back, then over the curve of my rear while running his stubbly chin over my neck. "Well, let me rekindle it again, my love."

∞∞∞∞

"Stop fussing. You look fine," I assured Tuck that afternoon.

In truth, he looked good enough to eat, and it was all I could do not to drag him into the nearest closet, strip, and screw him wildly.

He waggled his eyebrows, reading my mind. "Closet. Good idea."

I laughed. "That will have to wait. We have to rejoin our guests."

Our sensual morning was long past, and our wedding had gone beautifully. Even tough, no-nonsense Willa had hidden joyous tears. My father had cried too — openly, bless him — and even the king appeared to have something in his eye when Tuck and I had said *I do.*

I'd never been happier in my life. I'd never been more grateful either, because instead of mourning the tragic aftermath of Prince John's treachery, we were celebrating. All of Nottingham celebrated, a truly special sight to see.

At first, I'd worried about tying the knot in the very place we'd nearly lost our lives. But the town square had undergone an amazing transformation overnight, thanks to a man named Grove, who'd been nominated for the job by the sheriff.

He loves decorating, Daniel had assured us. *He just needs a little supervision.*

"Yes, sir. Out with the gallows, in with a happy wedding theme." Grove had nodded heartily when Daniel first presented the challenge. "I won't let you down."

And, wow. Grove had truly risen to the occasion. It was a beautiful, blue-sky winter's day, and the square had been decked out with pine boughs and flowers made of white cloth — a whole arched bower of them. I would never forget the long walk down that aisle with my father. Tuck's eyes never left mine as he waited by the altar. Willa and John were our maid of honor and best man, with the king, Robynne, and Daniel getting places of honor at the front of the ceremony.

I sighed to myself. All in all, the perfect wedding.

A feast was next on the agenda, but I had detoured to our room on the excuse of changing into a more practical dress. Obviously, I needed help with that, so I'd brought Tuck. Of course, one thing had led to another, and we'd ended up in bed again. But, hey. We were newlyweds. That was allowed, wasn't it?

But now, it *really* was time to rejoin our guests.

Tuck plucked at his sleeves. "I haven't worn anything but monks' robes in months. This could take some getting used to."

I laughed. "For me, too. But you look good. Really good."

Really, really good, my animal side hummed, tempting me with a side trip to that closet.

Tuck looked like an off-duty knight in those leather breeches and green tunic — a classy yet understated look I hoped would set the tone for our tenure as Lord and Lady of Nottingham. No over-the-top luxuries for us, just a lot of hard work and dedication to our core mission: laying the groundwork that would allow the people of Nottingham to live happy, peaceful lives.

I planted a firm kiss on Tuck's lips. "I promise to help you take them off again soon, dear husband."

His eyes sparkled, as I'm sure mine did. Would we ever get used to our wonderful new reality?

I pulled him in for another tight hug. "I couldn't have wished for a nicer wedding."

He nuzzled my cheek. "And the party's only just starting. Shall we?"

Chapter Twenty-Four

MARIAN

Tuck stuck out his elbow and led me out of the room, touching up his hair as he went.

I mussed it with an exasperated sigh. "Cats!"

He grinned. "I can't help it. Could be worse, though. It's not like I lick my—"

I stuck up a hand, stopping him there. I really, really didn't need the mental image of a cat twisting to clean its private parts.

"No need to share everything, dearest."

He grinned, leading me down the stairs to the packed banquet hall.

"A toast to the Lord and Lady of Nottingham!" someone called out as we entered.

Tuck and I peeked over our shoulders, ready to scurry out of their way. Then we caught ourselves and laughed.

"Oops. That's us." I grabbed Tuck's hand and towed him forward.

"Another thing I have to get used to," he murmured.

New and familiar faces greeted us from all sides, including Cyril the monk, who congratulated us heartily.

Tuck thumped him on the shoulder. "Congratulations."

Cyril's grin went even wider at that reference to his recent promotion.

"Me, acting librarian of the abbey! Can you believe it?"

I hid a smile. No. But someone had to fill the vacancy of Father Benedict, who'd been arrested as an accessory to treason.

Cyril pulled out a small package and presented it to me.

"We said no gifts," Tuck said.

"Not so much a gift as lost property," Cyril explained. "I found it in the library."

Tuck chuckled. "Lord, please don't let it be artwork..."

Cyril shushed him, turning red. "Artwork, but not mine."

I laughed upon opening the gift. "My needlepoint!"

Tuck laughed too, reading the half-finished proverb. "*She is clothed with strength and dignity; she can laugh at the days to come.* Very fitting."

I kissed Tuck, then thanked Cyril profusely. Not so much because I was dying to dig back into needlepoint, but for the reminder of the trials I'd survived over the past few weeks.

For the next hour, we made small talk with guests, quickly getting separated. I longed for Tuck back at my side, but I was almost as relieved when Robynne joined me.

"Apologies, but the king has asked for the lady of the house," she said, pulling me away from the crowd.

A fib, but she didn't seem the least bit rueful.

"Here." She steered me away and pressed a plate into my hand. "Wine. Bread. Cheese. You must be starving."

I was, though mostly from the... er, more physically demanding parts of my day. But, heck. Making love took energy. And when it came to sex with Tuck, lots and lots of energy.

"Food is great, but I'm mostly glad to talk to you — finally!" I said.

We'd had some time to chat the previous evening, and we'd hit it off immediately. Tuck was one rock that would keep me grounded here in Nottingham, and Robynne was another. I already knew I could count on her as a friend and adviser.

She smiled. "I agree. And the good thing is, that won't be so difficult now that we're neighbors."

Her grin said it all. Finally — finally! — she and Daniel could live and love each other openly. Robynne had already announced her move in to the sheriff's quarters and spent the previous night there. Judging by the rosy glow of her cheeks, she and Daniel had passed the hours in much the same way that Tuck and I had — naked and panting between the sheets.

Robynne's face went pink with sultry memories, and her eyes slid over to Daniel. Then she cleared her throat and led me to where he and Tuck were standing.

"Hello there," she said, taking Daniel's hand.

They kissed, then chuckled, still awash in the novelty of a public display of affection. Tuck pulled me in for a hug, squeezing me against his chest like he never wanted to let go. I closed my eyes, heartily agreeing with the sentiment.

"I thought I'd find you over by King Richard, listening to stories about his crusading adventures," I teased my husband.

Yes, *husband.* Every time I said or thought it, I grinned in delight.

Tuck shrugged and shot a grateful look at the sheriff.

"War doesn't have the appeal it used to. Besides, I have to get my mind around my new job."

"Don't worry," Daniel reassured him. "When I was first appointed sheriff, it felt like looking up an impossibly steep mountain. I'm still learning, but it's not the monster it used to be. Besides, I have faith in our new Lord of Nottingham."

When he raised his goblet to Tuck in a toast, Robynne and I exchanged amused looks. Up to now, those two had been uneasy allies at best. Now, their relationship seemed to be tipping toward *friendship.*

Don't look so surprised, Tuck whispered into my mind. *It's like you said. Miracles can happen.*

I squeezed his hand, echoing him. *Miracles can happen.*

"Still a bear of a job, but much more manageable," Daniel concluded.

Robynne glanced around the hall. "Speaking of bears, where are John and Willa?"

We all looked around. Most of the Merry Men were there, but not those two. I was just about to ask when the oak doors of the great hall were thrown open. Everyone looked up, and seconds later, cheers filled the room.

"John! Willa!"

I laughed. Talk about making a grand entrance. John strode up to the banquet table with a buck draped over his shoulders. Willa did the same, carrying a wild boar. When they both thumped their loads on the table, plates clattered, and wine slopped over the edge of many a goblet.

"A late wedding gift," Willa announced once we'd plowed through the crowd to greet them. "Seeing as you have so many guests to feed."

Nosewise was right on their heels, nearly bowling me over in his excitement.

I petted him. "Who's a good boy?"

I am, his whipping tail announced. Then he bounded over to Willa for more petting.

I sighed. I loved that dog, but it was clear he'd found the perfect home with Willa and John in Sherwood Forest.

Yes, Sherwood Forest. Robynne had decided to move to town, but John and Willa had chosen to remain in their camp in the woods.

You know, to keep an eye out for bandits, Willa had joked the previous evening.

"Thank you. We can definitely use more food. I never expected so many guests."

I motioned to the long line of well-wishers who filed in through one door and out another, picking up the fixings for their own feasts on the way. Some ate at the tables we'd squeezed into the banquet hall and adjoining corridors, while others ate in giant party tents erected in the town square.

"Damn good way to start winning over the people of Nottingham," Daniel observed.

"Tuck's idea," I admitted. "And a good one. But that's just the beginning."

We had already discussed more significant, long-term measures that would alleviate taxpayers while still financing public works that would benefit everybody. Cleaning up the streams that ran through town was one priority. Another was installing more public fountains to provide everyone with the modern convenience of clean, running water only a short walk from their homes. Truly amazing what luxuries the latest technology could bring.

Of course, we had only just started, but I felt like we were on the right track. And as for the feast, it was working. Many of the townsfolk were still wary of us, but the more they saw us as normal people and not crazed, wild animals, the more they would grow to trust us.

Not that I'd be revealing my unicorn to anyone. Only my true love, Tuck, whenever we could get away from our duties in the castle.

Robynne looked around the banquet hall, beaming. "Hard to believe this day has finally arrived. And you know what? I have a feeling people will tell their children and grandchildren about this happy day."

Tuck corrected her. "More than that. They'll tell legends — about you." Then he looped an arm around John's shoulders and joked, "Too bad no one will remember you, John Little."

The bear shifter shrugged. "Better than going down in history as Little John."

More chuckles ensued, though Robynne shook her head. "If there are legends, they'll be about all of us. You, you, and you." She pointed around, then sighed. "I just hope I don't go down in history as a man."

Willa and I groaned, while the men chuckled. Then we all clinked goblets.

"To Robynne Hood — female outlaw and master archer!"

Daniel pulled her in for a kiss. "Master archer *and* Nottingham's first alderwoman."

She grinned. "First of many, I hope."

We'd barely drunk a few sips when the king strode over with my father and Lord Winthrop.

"A buck. A boar," the king said flatly, pointing at the table.

Willa nodded proudly.

The king raised a bushy eyebrow. "Hunted in my private forest?"

Willa froze, then covered up with an innocent smile. "Oh no. Of course not. Wouldn't dream of it, sir."

The king harrumphed, and the other two men broke into laughter.

"We'd better deliver those to the kitchen," Willa said, scurrying away with John.

My father chuckled. "A good thing our king has a soft spot for capable ladies."

The king harrumphed again. "I have no soft spots."

I grinned. He did, but he hid them well. Not that I dared say as much.

Moments later, the king was swept away by a fresh group of admirers, but my father and Lord Winthrop lingered a little longer.

"So proud of you, dear girl." My father hugged me, then whispered, "Your mother would be proud too."

Tears welled in my eyes, but that was all right. It was nice to carry her memory with me on this special day.

My father cleared his throat and smacked Tuck's shoulder. "And you had better live up to expectations."

Tuck stuck on a polite, nervous smile. "I'll do my best, sir."

"A good place to start," Lord Winthrop agreed cheerily.

Lady Winthrop joined us next. "There you are, darlings. About your wedding gift..."

"You've already done so much for us," I protested.

"Nonsense, my dear girl. I have the perfect idea, especially now that you'll be living in this drafty castle."

"It's not that drafty," I protested, already feeling sentimental about the place.

I'd never aspired to be the leading lady in my own castle. But Nottingham called to me — plus, the job here gave me a real purpose.

"Oh, but it is," Lady Winthrop insisted. "Not to worry, however. We have the perfect gift for you, and with any luck, it will be delivered by next winter. Tell them, dear."

Lord Winthrop shook his head. "Your idea. You tell them." Then he turned to us. "She's the brains of the operation."

Tuck grinned and pointed to me. "So is she."

Lady Winthrop motioned to the wall. "We're commissioning a set of tapestries for you. Decorative *and* functional, since they'll cut down the draft. I was thinking of a unicorn and lion theme. You know, frolicking in fields of flowers..."

Tuck laughed, leaving me to reply with a broad grin. "I love it."

We chatted for a few more minutes until Lady Winthrop excused herself and towed her husband and my father to the king's table.

"Oh, they're serving that soup I adore..."

Next, Tuck was all but tackled by young Tom a moment later.

"Tuck! Tuck!"

"Lord Nottingham," someone corrected him, scandalized.

Tuck shook his head. "Tuck will do perfectly. How are you, Tom?"

"Fine. Full." He patted his belly then pointed at the high ceiling. "Do you really get to live in this castle?"

"Well, it comes with a big job, but yes. And you can visit any time you want."

"Can I bring my mother and sisters?"

My heart leaped out to him, as it had that day we'd visited the struggling family. I hoped today marked the beginning of better times for them and so many others. Then I corrected myself. I wouldn't just hope. I would work hard to make that a reality for all the people of Nottingham.

"You can all visit anytime," I assured him. "Now, if you don't mind, could you please make sure the cook doesn't mistake Nosewise for a deer and cook him?"

Tom laughed and ran off to play with the huge Great Dane.

"Enjoy the party!" Tuck called, then chuckled at a couple nestled closely at a side table, totally oblivious to the crowds. "I'll say *they're* enjoying it."

I laughed, because that was Bess and Robert, gazing lovingly into each other's eyes.

"I'm glad to see Bess with a good man," I whispered. "She deserves it."

Tuck laughed. "A month ago, I would have told you Robert wasn't up to the job. But I have to say, he's grown up. Maybe being a husband and stepfather is just what he needs to finish that process." Then he broke out laughing.

"What?" I tilted my head.

Tuck grinned. "I bet there are plenty of people who would say the same about me." He scratched his chest ruefully. "I just hope I'm up to the job."

I patted his arm. "Now that you're in the right job — yes, absolutely. And remember, you have me."

His eyes sparkled. "Speaking of which..."

He touched his heart, sending a shot of warmth through my body — and his, judging by the way his cheeks colored.

"Speaking of having me, you mean?" I teased in a husky whisper.

He pulled me flush against his body, whispering, "Yes. I'd like a replay of that unicorn bond, please. And maybe another bite."

When he nuzzled my neck, my pulse spiked.

"I'm sure our guests can take care of themselves while we take care of official business," he went on, kissing my neck. "Besides, tomorrow is our big day."

I laughed, slipping my hand inside his shirt. "I thought today was our big day."

He shook his head while inching his hands over my rear. "Tomorrow, we start our new jobs in earnest. And you know what they say..."

I waited. This, I had to hear.

"The key to good leadership is planning for a little *me* time."

I laughed, then corrected him. "*Us* time."

"A lifetime," he whispered, pulling me toward the stairs.

Epilogue

ROBYNNE

For about an hour after the king declared, *I believe a feast is in order,* I moved in a daze. So many emotions rushed through me at the same time that they tangled and stopped like sheep stuck at a narrow gate. All I really registered was Daniel's hand firmly around mine — punctuated by claps on my back from well-wishers. Not just from Willa, John, or the Merry Men, but from townsfolk, too.

"Robynne Hood! Robynne Hood!" they cheered.

Which was nice. Very nice. Right?

It ought to have been, but I didn't feel anything.

Some folks, I noticed through my mental haze, even bowed as Daniel and I passed on our way to congratulate Tuck and Marian.

Bowed — to me?

I moved stiffly, unsure what to do, say, or feel.

Thank goodness for Daniel steering me to his home in a nearby side street.

To change into something more suitable in the presence of the king, was his excuse.

Thank goodness for the privacy of his four walls, because the moment I sank to a chair, I broke down and sobbed.

And sobbed. . . and sobbed.

Yes, me, Robynne Hood, the cunning, unflappable outlaw, sobbing like a child. An endless fountain of tears burst forth, and there was no stopping them.

Tears for the silent, gut-wrenching goodbye Daniel and I had exchanged when we'd thought the end had come. Tears of dread as I pictured him sacrificing everything in a last-ditch effort to save me. Tears for the future we would never live and the child — or children — we would never hold.

And that was just the river of tears from that do-or-die moment in the town square. When that deluge passed, a second flood overwhelmed me — one for everything we'd endured in the time leading up to today. Months of fear, frustration, and separation as Daniel and I filled incompatible roles as sheriff and outlaw, hiding our forbidden love. Tears for the interminable years before that, too, when I'd mourned, believing Daniel dead.

Through all that time, I'd held the tears back. Forever, or so I'd thought.

Apparently, though, sorrow didn't dry up like a puddle. It collected, hidden in some deep, dark place. Filling quietly... waiting until the day something snapped and it could all gush forth.

Daniel sat beside me, holding me. Not trying to stem my tears, just holding me through it all.

At some point, I shuddered and heaved a deep breath. There. I was done.

Then I started crying again, a whole new flavor this time. Tears of joy and relief now — the kind where you replayed a great stroke of luck again and again, unable to process your own good fortune.

We'd survived — not only Daniel and I, but everyone else. We'd rid the world of a small evil, and best of all, we no longer had to hide our love.

"Can you believe it?" I managed to whisper at some point.

Daniel flashed the biggest, happiest, freest smile I'd ever seen on him. "Yes. I believe. I always did. I always will." He kissed me. "I believe in you and me."

Just when I'd finally finished crying...

"Damn you, Sheriff," I cursed him softly. "You've set me off again."

He laughed, then tipped my chin up. "Not just you. Look."

I blinked through the curtain of my tears, then caught my breath. Two wet streaks glistened down my true love's face, then collected in the reservoir of the smile beneath.

∞∞∞∞

That night, we lay in bed, holding each other close. Whispering, touching, marveling at everything that had transpired. In the morning, we made slow, sweet love, so unlike the whirlwind I had always imagined if our day finally came.

Maybe we were still reeling inside. Maybe we were older and wiser, because a single day could age a person as much as ten years. Either way, we drew out every kiss, every slow, burning touch, and every needy groan in that slow dance to an unforgettable high.

Afterward, we basked in our own heat, then chuckled, just because.

"When is that wedding again?" Daniel asked at some point.

I grinned. "You mean Tuck and Marian's or ours?"

He flashed another huge, sunny smile and kissed me. "Theirs. For now."

Prophetic words, because four months after Tuck and Marian's big day, we held a smaller, quieter celebration of our own. Not in town, but under the oaks of Sherwood Forest.

"Don't you look a picture." John Little smiled at us both.

I turned from side to side, letting my dress swish. "Cement this moment into your mind, my dear bear, because this may be the last time you see me look this good."

"It's the flowers," Willa joked, touching the wreath on my head, then hers.

She'd made both, using the prettiest of the spring flowers that seemed to bloom everywhere now that winter had given way to spring and spring was knocking on summer's door. She'd even made one for Daniel.

"Sorry, ladies. I think mine is the best," he chuckled, touching his headdress.

"I think we all look good," Robert said, flicking his messier flower necklace.

All the Merry Men wore one of those — as did Sausage, George, and Connie, the camp dogs. But Robert's was the best, because Bess's children had made it for him.

Whose children? he growled into my mind.

I chuckled. *Sorry. Your children.*

His eyes slid to Bess's belly, and he puffed his chest out a little. *All four.*

Yes, my exasperating, bumbling brother was a young father now, with Bess's three plus a fourth on its way. And I had to hand it to him — he was doing a fine job as doting dad and loving partner. I'd never seen him — or Bess — look happier. They lived on her farm on the edge of the forest, where they had been working hard to make the coming harvest a plentiful one.

"You do look good. Both of you," my father said, looping one arm around Robert and the other around me.

I leaned into him, closing my eyes. My father had always been our rock and our role model, demanding the highest standards from us both—

Okay, higher standards for me than dear, dimwitted Robert, but still...

—so I'd spent many a sleepless night worrying about what he would think of my life as an outlaw.

"I'm so proud." He kissed the top of my head, then Robert's. "Your mother would be too."

"You think so?" Robert sniffed quietly.

"I know so," my father said.

The three of us held each other for a while. Then a couple of small, thin arms joined in from behind, and I peeked down to find Bess's son, Tom.

"There's my boy," Robert cheered, lifting him and spinning him around.

"My boy too," my father whispered, watching them both.

A good thing I was all cried out by then, so only a happy lump formed in my throat. Whew.

I looked at Robert, my father, and Daniel. Then I looked around the beautiful forest camp that had once been my home.

I loved my new life in Nottingham, but Sherwood Forest would forever hold a special place in my heart.

I looked at my friends next, gathered together for this happy occasion. As always, I was awed at how well things had worked out.

"Can I tempt you with the abbey's finest brew, Mr. Hood?" Tuck broke into my reverie, coming up with two frothy mugs.

No man would ever hold a candle to Daniel in my eyes, but damn, did Tuck cut a fine figure as a noble lord — a down-to-earth, cheery lord who'd won the hearts of the people of Nottingham after only a few months on the job.

Well, he'd had the women's hearts from day one. But most men had expressed their grudging approval by now too.

"Don't mind if I do." My father took a mug, clinked with Tuck, and downed his drink in one gulp. He hadn't become Locksley's armorer by being a lightweight. Then he stuck an elbow toward me. "Shall we?"

I looped my arm through his and grinned at Daniel. "Ready if you are."

Daniel popped a kiss on my lips, then hurried to the leafy altar the men had built under Major Oak. My father and I made my way there slowly, letting everyone take their places.

I'd thoroughly enjoyed Marian and Tuck's wedding, but our small, intimate service suited us perfectly. Instead of a choir, we had chirping birds. Instead of the soaring ceiling of a church, we had the interlocking branches of oaks. And instead of an aisle lined with pews, we had a faint path lined with flowers.

Yes, the Merry Men had gone all out for the occasion, commanded, no doubt, by Willa's firm hand.

We'd asked Tuck to preside over the ceremony, if not as a man of the cloth then as Lord of Nottingham. He refused as politely as he could.

Not on my life — nothing personal! — but I know the perfect man for the job...

Thus, it wasn't Tuck behind the altar, but Friar Cyril.

A man of, er, interesting talents, as Tuck had put it.

My father hugged me again, then wiped his right eye — dust, no doubt — and nudged me toward Daniel. I clasped his hands and lost myself in my true love's beautiful blue eyes.

"Dearly beloved..." Cyril started.

Marian, not far to my left, sighed happily and laced her fingers through Tuck's.

Bess held her younger daughter and gazed lovingly at Robert, who returned the look.

Willa and John did the same. Nosewise, the Great Dane, slobbered happily at the sight of so many of his favorite people gathered in one place. The other camp dogs were on their best behavior too, sensing a special occasion... or hopeful for treats in the feast that would follow.

"We are gathered here today..." Cyril went on.

Daniel's eyes shone, twin seas sparkling under a brilliant sun. So brightly, I lost myself there, making the rest of the ceremony fade to the background.

A ceremony that Cyril might have drawn out a little too long, because I caught Tuck signaling for him to move things along.

"Et cetera, et cetera," the monk concluded. "Now, if there are no objections—"

A huge body hurtled forward, and everyone gasped, then laughed.

"Nosewise," I scolded as the Great Dane jumped at me.

Daniel rolled his eyes, but Robert saved the day.

"Over here, Nosey." He patted his legs, coaxing the dog over and rewarding him with a thorough patting. "Who'sagoodboy?"

Daniel cleared his throat impatiently, but it came out like a dragon growl. Cyril cringed, then hurried on.

"Do you, Robynne Hood—"

"I do," I blurted, beating him to it.

"Do you, Daniel Cook—"

"I do," Daniel cut in.

Everyone chuckled, including Cyril.

"You may now— Oh my."

I wasn't looking at the time, but Marian joked afterward at the crimson Cyril had blushed when Daniel and I fell into a deep, passionate kiss.

A kiss for the ages, because boy, did we deserve it.

I'm not sure when we broke apart, or if we ever did. I remember a party springing up around us, though, much like those blossoms in the fields. I remember the crackling bonfire, the laughs, the jokes. But most of all, I remember the feeling of peace in my soul. And not just peace making a brief visit, but settling in for good.

"Can life really be this good?" I whispered to Daniel.

He smoothed a stray lock of hair into place under my flowery wreath. "It can. It is."

I hugged him tightly, sending a dozen *I love yous* into his mind.

Daniel held me just as tightly, whispering in my ear. "You remember that day at Poor Knight's Castle? When things looked so bleak, but we hung on?"

I nodded, growing somber.

He tipped my chin up, letting his smile jump over to me. "We're there now. We made it."

We made it, my fox side sighed joyously.

"So much has changed, but I'll still live by those words," Daniel vowed, then echoed what he'd said on that day. "From this moment on, we'll savor every minute we spend together. Because those better days we wished for — they're here now."

My fox wagged her tail, hinting at a more...er, intimate way to ring in this new chapter in our lives. Daniel's eyes sparkled, telling me his dragon was on board with that plan.

I let my hands drift down his rear at the same time his snuck up my ribs.

"Better days, indeed," I whispered, kissing his ear. "With many more to come."

Sneak Peek: Fire Maidens: Paris

Paris! City of dreams — or shifter nightmares?

Natalie Brewer has come to Paris to live out a dream, not a nightmare. Then a vampire attack exposes her to a whole new side to the City of Lights — and to her own heritage. Before she knows it, she's swept into a world she never imagined, with gargoyles, werewolves, and dragons who claim she's descended from a legendary shifter queen. Now her life is in danger, and it's impossible to know who to trust, other than the mysterious stranger who risks his life for her again and again.

After a decade in the Foreign Legion, all dragon shifter Tristan Chevalier wants is to settle into a civilian life and a new job. His mission: to prove himself to the Guardians of Paris and to protect the city. But all that is threatened when an innocent woman stumbles into his life — and into his heart. Being appointed her bodyguard is a blessing and a curse, because Natalie is absolutely, positively off-limits despite the smoldering desire they both feel. Worse, every shifter in Paris has set their sights on her, from bloodthirsty vampires to power-hungry dragons and jealous rivals. For Tristan, it's the test of a lifetime, and the outcome will affect the fortunes of an entire city.

Books by Anna Lowe

Sherwood Forest Shifters

Tempting the Sheriff (Book 1)

Tempting the Outlaw (Book 2)

Tempting the Maiden (Book 3)

Aloha Shifters - Jewels of the Heart

Lure of the Dragon (Book 1)

Lure of the Wolf (Book 2)

Lure of the Bear (Book 3)

Lure of the Tiger (Book 4)

Love of the Dragon (Book 5)

Lure of the Fox (Book 6)

Aloha Shifters - Pearls of Desire

Rebel Dragon (Book 1)

Rebel Bear (Book 2)

Rebel Lion (Book 3)

Rebel Wolf (Book 4)

Rebel Heart (A prequel to Book 5)

Rebel Alpha (Book 5)

Fire Maidens - Billionaires & Bodyguards

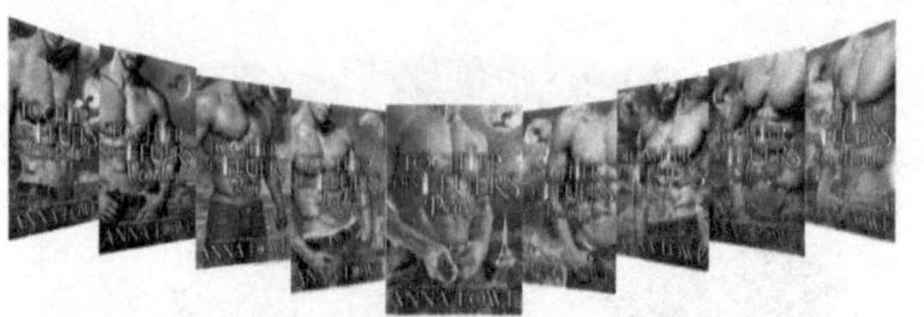

Fire Maidens: Paris (Book 1)

Fire Maidens: London (Book 2)

Fire Maidens: Rome (Book 3)

Fire Maidens: Portugal (Book 4)

Fire Maidens: Ireland (Book 5)

Fire Maidens: Scotland (Book 6)

Fire Maidens: Venice (Book 7)

Fire Maidens: Greece (Book 8)

Fire Maidens: Switzerland (Book 9)

The Wolves of Twin Moon Ranch

Desert Hunt (the Prequel)

Desert Moon (Book 1)

Desert Blood (Book 2)

Desert Fate (Book 3)

Desert Heart (Book 4)

Desert Rose (Book 5)

Desert Roots (Book 6)

Desert Destiny (Book 7)

Sasquatch Surprise (Book 8)

Desert Yule (a short story)

Desert Wolf: Complete Collection (Four short stories)

Blue Moon Saloon

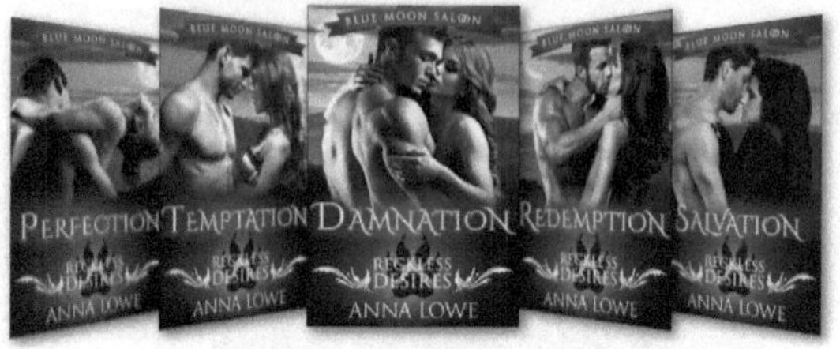

Perfection (a short story prequel)

Damnation (Book 1)

Temptation (Book 2)

Redemption (Book 3)

Salvation (Book 4)

Deception (Book 5)

Celebration (a holiday treat)

Shifters in Vegas

Paranormal romance with a zany twist

Gambling on Trouble

Gambling on Her Dragon

Gambling on Her Bear

Gambling on Her Panther

Serendipity Adventure Romance

Off the Charts

Uncharted

Entangled

Windswept

Adrift

Travel Romance

Veiled Fantasies

Island Fantasies

www.annalowebooks.com

About the Author

USA Today and Amazon bestselling author Anna Lowe loves putting the "hero" back into heroine and letting location ignite a passionate romance. She likes a heroine who is independent, intelligent, and imperfect – a woman who is doing just fine on her own. But give the heroine a good man – not to mention a chance to overcome her own inhibitions – and she'll never turn down the chance for adventure, nor shy away from danger.

Anna loves dogs, sports, and travel – and letting those inspire her fiction. On any given weekend, you might find her hiking in the mountains or hunched over her laptop, working on her latest story. Either way, the day will end with a chunk of dark chocolate and a good read.

Visit AnnaLoweBooks.com

www.ingramcontent.com/pod-product-compliance
Lightning Source LLC
Chambersburg PA
CBHW030754190726
48285CB00003B/855